Fireflies

Ally Blue

A Samhain publishing, Ltd. publication.

Samhain Publishing, Ltd.
577 Mulberry Street, Suite 1520
Macon, GA 31201
www.samhainpublishing.com

Fireflies
Copyright © 2008 by Ally Blue
Print ISBN: 978-1-59998-786-6
Digital ISBN: 1-59998-529-2

Editing by Sasha Knight
Cover by Anne Cain

First Samhain Publishing, Ltd. electronic publication: July 2007
First Samhain Publishing, Ltd. print publication: May 2008

Dedication

To Jet, J.L., Willa, Kimber and Luisa, the best crit group ever! I love you guys!

Prologue

"Mama!" Joey raced into the kitchen as fast as his five-year-old legs would carry him, letting the screen door slam in his excitement. "Mama, guess what?"

"Joseph Robert Vines, how many times have I told you not to slam the door?" Mama frowned over her shoulder, hands still busy in the sink full of dirty dishes. "Goodness sake, boy, wipe your feet. They're filthy."

Joey ran back and swiped his bare feet halfheartedly on the mat. "Mama, there's a man outside, and he says he can do magic. I know I ain't s'posed to talk to strangers, but he was real nice and he said he could show me lots of cool stuff. I told him I gotta ask you first, though. Can I go back outside so me and him can play? Please, Mama?"

The plate Mama was washing slipped out of her hands, splashing soapy water all over the floor. She whirled around. "What?"

"I was outside catchin' fireflies, and he just appeared, like that Jeannie lady on TV. He said he's a faery, and he can do all sorts of cool magic." Joey blinked up at his mother. Her soft brown skin had turned a weird color, kind of like the mud in Sawyer's Swamp outside town. "You sick, Mama?"

She didn't answer. Running across the room, Mama shut and locked the wooden door, then knelt beside Joey and laid her hands on his shoulders. "What'd this man look like, Joey?"

"He was real pretty. All white and shiny, even his hair. Like one of the angels at church. And he didn't have no clothes on. And," Joey added, with the emphasis he felt this particular bit deserved, "he had wings."

Mama made a funny sort of sound. "Baby, did he hurt you? Did he?"

"No, ma'am." Joey felt his lip start to tremble as he sensed Mama's fear. "I didn't do nothin' wrong."

Mama stared at him like she didn't hear him. She looked even more scared than she had that time when he had the pneumonia and almost died. He'd never seen his mama look like that. Tears started to spill down his cheeks, his breath hitching.

"Oh. Oh, baby. Come here." Mama opened her arms and Joey flung himself into them, letting her soothe and comfort him. "It's okay, honey. It's okay. Mama's not mad at you." She pushed him back enough to look him in the face. "But I want you to listen to me real good. Okay?"

Joey sniffed deeply and nodded. He felt ashamed that he'd cried. He was too big to cry. "Yes, ma'am."

Mama's face was very serious. "There's no such thing as faeries. That man you saw isn't a faery, and he can't do magic. He's just a man. A sick man who likes to take little boys and do bad things to them."

"But, Mama, what about...?"

She stopped him, almost like she knew what he was going to say. *What about the wings, Mama?* "You got a strong imagination, Joseph. You always did. Got that from..." Mama stopped and took a deep breath. "Got it from your daddy."

Joey almost laughed. He loved his daddy, but Mama was wrong. Daddy didn't have any imagination at all. Mama got a strange look on her face, one he'd seen before when she thought he wasn't watching. He choked back his laughter and tried to look serious. "Yes, ma'am."

She smiled gently at him. "You run on up to bed now. Keep your window shut and locked, you hear?"

"Yes, ma'am."

He let Mama hug him and kiss his cheek, then bounded up the stairs, calling "good night" over his shoulder. He brushed his teeth, headed into his room and changed into his pajamas. Door shut behind him, lights off, he opened the window in blatant disregard of his mother's orders and leaned his elbows on the sill. The night air felt cool on his face. Out in the field, the fireflies twinkled in the dusk. One of them wasn't quite what it seemed. Maybe all of them.

It didn't matter what Mama said about it. He wasn't a baby anymore. He knew what was real, and what wasn't. With one last curious glance at the fireflies, he climbed into bed and closed his eyes.

C03

Daddy came home from his overnight delivery run the next morning. Mama sent Joey to his room the minute he finished breakfast. She and Daddy had to have a talk, she said.

Joey knew what that meant. In his room, he left the door open a crack and sat on the floor listening to Mama and Daddy fight. Mama wanted to move someplace with a lot of people, like a big city. Maybe California somewhere. She didn't think Fontaine, Louisiana was safe anymore.

That didn't make any sense to Joey. Fontaine was the sort of place where everyone knew everyone else and nobody locked their doors. Mama had said so herself lots of times. He didn't understand why she thought a big city would be safer than Fontaine, when she'd always said Fontaine was the safest place there could be.

Daddy said pretty much what Joey was thinking, then said they couldn't afford to move anyhow and that was that. Mama called him a heartless bastard, Daddy called her a crazy bitch, then they both said they were sorry and Mama cried.

Grownups were so silly sometimes.

The faery came to his room that night. Soon as he saw the firefly outside his window, he knew it was his new friend. He didn't know *how* he knew, he just *knew*.

He pushed the window open. The firefly floated inside. There was a soft bluish pulse of light, and suddenly the firefly was gone and the faery stood there, the ends of his wings trailing the floor.

Joey stared in awe at the creature's face. He thought the faery was the prettiest thing ever, even prettier than his mama, and she was more beautiful than a movie star.

The faery smiled and took a step toward him, white skin shining in the moonlight, long cottony hair floating in the light breeze. "Hello, Joseph." The faery's lilting voice made Joey think of bells. "I'm so happy to see you again."

"Mama says you ain't a faery," Joey said. "She says you can't do magic or nothin', that you're a sick man who wants to do bad things to me."

The faery's smile faded a little. "Do you believe that?"

Joey considered. "Nope. A man don't have wings, so I figure you must be a faery like you said." He tilted his head, eyeing the long, sheer wings with curiosity. "Those real?"

He got a smile and a gentle laugh. "Yes, they are. You can touch them, if you like."

Joey edged cautiously forward, reached out and ran his fingertips along the edge of one wing. It felt soft, but strong, sort of like spider silk without the stickiness. "Wow," he breathed, stroking the sheer wing a little more boldly. "It's really real."

"Yes, indeed."

"Can you fly with 'em?"

"I most certainly can." The faery smiled. "Will you come with me, Joseph? Maybe I'll teach you to fly too, one day."

Joey felt torn. He wanted to see where the faery lived. And learning to fly would be cool, even though he didn't see how he was going to fly without wings. But his mama had looked so scared. Besides, she needed him to stay with her. Some people in town were mean to her because she was black and Daddy was white. Daddy said those people were backward hicks and she shouldn't pay them any mind, but it still hurt her feelings, Joey could tell. It would break her heart if he left her alone, with no one to protect her when Daddy was off working.

"I better not," he said after a while. "Mama needs me."

Some of the light seemed to go out of the faery's silvery eyes, but he nodded anyway. "Of course. Stay and look after your mother."

"Will you ever come back?" Joey asked, hoping he would say yes.

The faery ran his fingers down Joey's cheek. The touch made Joey's stomach flutter strangely. "Never fear. I'll come back for you, when you're ready." He leaned down, so close Joey could feel warm breath against his ear. "Remember me, Joseph."

He kissed Joey's forehead, whispering something soft and musical against his skin, then stepped back. The blue light pulsed, and there was a little firefly again, the faery gone like a dream. Joey watched the firefly flutter out into the night. He brushed his fingers over the spot where his friend had kissed him. The skin there tingled.

"I'll remember," he promised.

Chapter One

"Okay, you ready?"

Joey took a deep breath and let it out slowly. "Let's do it."

Matt laughed in his slightly unhinged way. "All right, here we go."

The buzz of the tattoo needle cut through the music from the CD player. Joey willed his body to relax against the plastic-covered padding of the tattoo chair he straddled. He gazed out the window at the sunny little courtyard as the needle etched his lifelong vision into the flesh of his back. This was his eighth and final sitting. Matt only had the top parts left to finish. After today, Joey would finally have his wings.

Years ago, Joey had tried to convince himself what he'd seen as a child wasn't real. But it hadn't worked. He knew what he'd seen. The encounter was crystal clear in his mind, even after twenty years. Whenever Joey closed his eyes, he saw the faery's shining white skin, heard his gentle voice. He'd felt the ghost of that soft kiss on his forehead for days afterward.

Maybe it had only been the product of a five-year-old boy's overactive imagination. But it had felt more real than anything ever had, before or since. And he'd never stopped wanting the wings.

"Hey, Joey?"

He shook himself out of his daydream with an effort. "Hm?"

"Why faery wings?"

Matt had never asked him that before, not even during the days they'd spent working on the design for the tattoo, Joey fumbling for the vocabulary to explain what he wanted and Matt producing sketch after sketch until he got it exactly right.

Joey smiled. "Just something I dreamed once."

⁓

Three hours later, Joey shrugged gingerly into his shirt, trying not to disturb the plastic wrap covering the upper part of his back. He felt light and giddy. What he'd seen reflected in the mirror was closer to the wings of his childhood memory than he'd dreamed possible. Delicate tracings in pale green, ice blue and silvery white, springing from between his shoulder blades, spreading across his back and shoulders and trailing down over his buttocks, with the tapered tips curling down the backs of his legs all the way to his ankles. Against the creamy café au lait of his skin, the effect was stunning.

"You know the drill," Matt said, stripping off his gloves and tossing them into the trash. "Wash three times a day with mild soap and coat it with antibiotic ointment for three days. Then use unscented lotion a couple times a day until it's healed."

"Sure thing." Joey held a hand out. "This is amazing work, Matt, thanks."

Matt flashed a wide, dimpled grin as he shook Joey's hand. "Hell, I should be thanking you. I fucking loved doing this tat. Hey, you're gonna come back and let me see it after it's all healed, right? I want to take some pics."

"Sure thing." Joey dug his wallet out of his jeans pocket. "Three hundred?"

"Yeah."

Joey counted out the money and handed it to Matt. "There. And I even have enough left for a coffee."

"You do? Damn, I must not be charging enough."

Joey laughed. "See you later, Matt. Thanks again."

"Yeah, see you."

Joey left the shop grinning from ear to ear. The wings had taken months to do and cost him two thousand dollars he really couldn't spare, but it was worth it. Having the wings made him feel complete in a way he couldn't describe.

Almost complete, he mentally amended as he walked toward the coffee shop two doors down from Dragon's Den Tattoo and Piercing. His gut told him he'd never be truly whole inside until the faery found him again.

And what then? He had no idea. But he'd waited most of his life to find out.

Satan's Brew was as crowded and noisy as ever. The couches and tiny tables were packed with people drinking espresso or chai tea and commenting on the paintings by local artists hanging on the black walls. Joey made his way through the usual crowd of goths, hippies and eccentric retirees to the counter. A girl with purple ponytails and a sweet smile poured him his usual organic fair trade dark roast. He mixed in a little bit of soy milk, put a plastic lid on the cup and headed back out into the cool of an early May evening.

Strolling down the street and sipping his coffee, Joey thought back to his first days in Asheville. Mama hadn't wanted him to move here, and at first he'd thought she was right. He'd missed Louisiana terribly, the sights and sounds and smells of his hometown that were as familiar to him as his own reflection. Then he'd found work at a nursery specializing in exotic plants, he'd discovered Asheville's eclectic art and music scene, and he'd found his rhythm. He'd been here nearly five years, and he hadn't missed his childhood home in a long time.

Sometimes, though, in the quiet moments, he was struck by the fear that his faery friend was looking for him and couldn't find him. He hadn't forgotten the faery's promise any more than he'd forgotten the silky feel of the creature's lips on his skin. *I'll come back for you, when you're ready.*

He stopped at the next corner and stared at the tiny park across the street. Fireflies blinked in the dimness under the trees, alluring and mysterious.

"I've got my wings now," he whispered. "Am I ready yet?"

The fireflies declined to answer. Turning his back on the park and its silent inhabitants, Joey headed off to catch the bus home.

ଓ

Joey got off the bus at the corner of Merrimon and University and walked the remaining mile and a half to his apartment, as he usually did. The small, well-kept building was situated a little ways up a narrow, curving road a stone's throw from the UNC-A campus. Scents of flowers and new leaves perfumed the air. Joey breathed deep as he strolled through the dusk, soaking up the feeling of vibrant life all around him.

Inside, Joey tossed his keys on the table beside the door and wandered over to the window, shedding his clothes as he went. The wide sheet of clear cellophane protecting his newly tattooed skin stayed on, held in place by a few pieces of tape. Joey breathed a sigh of relief as he kicked his underwear aside and stretched, wincing at the burn in his back. He'd always felt most comfortable nude, which he figured was one reason he could never keep a roommate.

Pulling the curtains aside, he looked out over the wide lawn and thick forested patch behind the building. The trees formed a deeper darkness against the indigo sky. A pair of children whose family lived downstairs from him ran laughing through the grass. It was a wonderfully peaceful scene, bringing back memories of a childhood spent mostly outdoors.

The thought of those long-ago days made his chest tight. Turning from the window, Joey fished through the desk drawer until he found his cell phone and dialed his mother's number. No one answered, and Joey cursed under his breath. *She shouldn't be working tonight.* He cut the connection before the answering machine could pick up, then punched in the numbers for Duvall's Jewelry in Fontaine, where his mother worked.

"Duvall's, this is Evangeline speaking, what can I do for you this evening?"

Joey smiled. His mother still refused to say "How may I direct your call?" claiming it sounded cold and impersonal. "Hi, Mama."

"Joey! How are you, baby?"

"I'm fine. What about you? I called home but you weren't there, so I figured you must be working."

"Yes. Jane, Sarah and I are closing the shop tonight."

Frowning, Joey shifted the phone to his other ear and picked up his small watering can from the shelf by the window where he kept his plant care supplies. "Why can't someone else do it?" he wondered, going to water the

African violets lining his windowsill. "Don't they know this isn't a good night for you?"

His mother sighed. "I'd rather work than sit at home by myself, missing him."

Joey's throat constricted, thinking of the day precisely three years ago when his mother had called and told him his father had been killed in an accident. He'd fallen asleep at the wheel of his delivery truck and it had run off the road. The shock of it still resonated in Joey's heart. Joey and his father had often been at odds, but they'd always loved each other, and Joey missed him.

Blinking away the sting of tears, Joey began watering the violets one by one. "Is Albert going to come stay with you tonight? I worry about you being alone."

"Goodness, no," his mother exclaimed, clearly scandalized by the idea of the man she was dating staying the night. "But I'm off tomorrow, so he's going to take me on a picnic. He thinks it'll be good for me to get out."

"He's right." Setting the watering can down, Joey stroked the leaves of a lush white violet with a gentle touch. The feel of the cool greenery against his skin soothed him. "Okay, well, I don't want you to get in trouble for personal calls so I'll go now. I just wanted to check on you."

"Now you know the Duvalls don't mind you calling me, especially tonight. And I'm glad you called, honey. I know you've found your place there in Asheville, but I do miss having you around."

"I miss you too, Mama," Joey answered, smiling into the phone. "Have fun on the picnic tomorrow, and tell Albert I said hi."

"I surely will, sweetheart. Oh, Joseph?"

"Yeah?" Joey picked up the watering can again and headed for the hanging basket of multicolored Lobelia in the corner.

"How have you been, honey? Is everything all right?"

The strange thread of hesitancy in his mother's voice, almost as if she were hiding something, sent a shiver of unease through Joey's bones. "Yeah, everything's fine. Why?"

"Just asking after my son's happiness, that's all. Can't a mother wonder how her baby's doing?"

Joey frowned. His mother sounded tense and a bit shrill, which was not like her at all. "Mama? What's going on? Is there something you're not telling me?"

"Not at all," she answered, her tone screaming the exact opposite. "Just...you be sure and call if you need me, okay? Any time."

"I will." Standing on tiptoe, Joey trickled water onto the Lobelia's roots. "Are you sure you—"

"I'm fine, baby," she interrupted. "I'll talk to you soon. I love you."

"Love you too. Mama—"

The phone clicked, and Joey was left listening to the sound of a dead connection. He pulled the phone away from his ear and stared at it, his insides churning. His mother hadn't acted this strange and secretive in ages. Not since the weeks following the faery's visit. Young though he'd been, Joey had immediately realized she was lying when she said the creature was no more than a disturbed man. She'd known what he was, but hadn't wanted to admit it to Joey.

When the faery failed to return, Joey's mother had relaxed into her old self again and stopped pleading with Joey's father to move to another state. Joey had learned not to mention the incident, or to give any hint of his secret hope of seeing the faery again. In all the years since, they'd never acknowledged what they both knew to be true. Joey couldn't help wondering if his mother's unusual behavior tonight was her way of attempting to start talking about it.

He hoped so. It was no hardship to avoid telling his friends and coworkers he'd been waiting twenty years for a mythical creature to find him and somehow fill the empty space in his life. But keeping himself from talking to his mother about it was hard. She knew, yet didn't want him to know she knew, and Joey was tired of dancing around it. He wished they could just bring the whole thing out in the open finally. He'd have given anything to know how his mother knew about faeries being real, and what had happened to make her fear them so.

Sighing, Joey set the phone on the desk and went back to caring for his plants. After a while, he lost himself in the familiar routine, and his worries about his mother settled to the back of his mind.

He chattered to his plants as he wandered naked through the apartment watering roots and pinching off dead blossoms. His last boyfriend used to tease him about his penchant for looking after his roomful of plants in the nude. Joey had laughed, then gone ahead and done it anyway. It felt right to him, and he'd never been one to question his instincts.

As he worked, his imagination conjured an image of a man working alongside him, naked as Joey was, but tall and pale with silver-gray eyes and flowing white hair. And wings. Long gossamer wings that trailed the floor and slid silky soft across his skin.

He smiled. *Can't forget the wings.*

CB

June came sweeping in like a dragon, breathing fire across the mountains. The old folks swore they'd never known such heat there, with the mercury topping ninety-five degrees day after breathless day. Crops shriveled and the water level in the lakes and rivers crept relentlessly down as each new day dawned hot and cloudless.

Joey imagined he could feel the earth thirsting for the rain that never came. Sometimes at night, he dreamed the trees and withered flowers were whispering to him, begging for relief from the drought. He'd wake up panting and sweating, heart racing with a fear that seemed to come from outside himself. It even seeped into his waking life, filling him with a vague but constant anxiety.

The feeling grew into an overwhelming restlessness. He woke on the morning of Midsummer's Eve with a smothering sense of something huge hanging over him. It crawled under his skin like a swarm of insects. Even the nursery, where he usually felt the most peaceful, wasn't a refuge from it.

"Joey, honestly," his boss said the third time Joey dropped the pruning scissors. "What's wrong with you today?"

"Sorry, Miranda." Sighing, Joey set the scissors on the work table and leaned against it. "I don't know. I'm jumpy for some reason. Maybe there's a storm coming or something."

Miranda pursed her lips, and Joey bit back a laugh. His rather uncanny ability to predict the weather based on his own physical and emotional state had always disturbed her. She was a mountain woman, born and raised, but unlike most Appalachian natives she scorned the idea that human beings had an intrinsic link with the natural world.

"Well, if there's rain coming, it's hiding pretty damn well. Not a cloud in the sky, as usual." Brushing back a strand of snow-white hair, which had come loose from her bun to fall in her eyes, she pulled off her work gloves and set them on the metal table. "I'm going out front. Ellen should be here soon with that shipment of bone meal, and Wayne's off today so I'll need to help unload it."

"I can do that," Joey offered. "It's only been a few months since your back surgery."

Miranda smiled. "Thanks, honey, but the doc said I can lift as long as it's no more than one bag at a time. Besides, I need you in here. The Zygopetalums need watering, and you're the only one I got who can do it right. Everybody else gives 'em too much."

"You can do it right," Joey pointed out, crossing his arms and giving her a stern look. "This is how you ruptured that disc in the first place, you know, lifting giant bags of bone meal."

"As hot and dry as it's been lately, our orchids are suffering, even here in the greenhouse, and the Zygopetalums seem to have it the worst. You have a way with them nobody else has, not even me." She patted his shoulder with one gnarled, soil-stained hand. "Don't worry about my back. I swear I'll be careful."

Joey shook his head as she bustled out of the greenhouse, heading for the nursery. There was no reasoning with her; her business came first, always. Which was probably why Miranda's Exotics was *the* place in Asheville to find rare and exotic plants.

Of course, he'd much rather care for the orchids than unload supplies, and Miranda knew that. Even though she scoffed at the idea of plants responding to certain people more than others, there was no denying all the plants' health improved when Joey was the one looking after them. Miranda attributed it to a combination of skill, knowledge and natural talent. Joey knew better. He'd never studied, never cultivated any skills. All he had to do was spend a few minutes with a plant, and he instinctively knew what it needed to thrive. He couldn't

25

explain it, and felt no need to. It was his particular gift, his calling, and he was content with that.

Shaking himself, Joey picked up the watering can and headed into the depths of the greenhouse. He had orchids to water.

CB

The afternoon passed in a blur for Joey. His hands went through the familiar routine of watering, feeding and assessing the condition of the various plants, but his mind refused to stay focused. The sense of impending doom he'd wrestled with all day sharpened into near panic, drowning out everything else. The air crackled with it. His body felt like a pressure cooker about to blow.

Just as he finished feeding the Bird of Paradise plants, a sudden wave of dizziness washed over him, setting his head whirling. The world spun around him. He clutched at the bench full of tropical flowers, almost knocking one over, and managed to keep from falling down.

Swallowing nausea, he lowered himself to the ground and leaned his forehead against his knees. *Maybe I picked up that virus Wayne had.* So far, everyone at Miranda's except him had suffered through it. *Maybe that's why I've felt so weird today.*

Part of him argued against that theory, but Joey didn't want to listen to that part. Blaming his strange state of mind on a virus was easier than believing the voice in his head telling him his life was about to change in ways he couldn't even imagine.

He heard the greenhouse door open and close. Miranda came into view a few seconds later. Her hazel eyes widened when she saw him.

"What's the matter, Joey? You don't look so good." She knelt beside Joey and laid a hand on his forehead. "You feel a little warm, too. Hope you're not catching that bug that's been going around."

"Yeah, that's what I was just thinking." Joey wiped a dew of sweat from his upper lip. "Damn. I had plans for tonight." He didn't mention that his plans consisted of sneaking into the Biltmore Estate grounds, hiking deep into the woods and watching the stars sparkle through a shroud of leaves.

"Well, whatever it was, it can wait." Rising to her feet, Miranda grasped Joey's hand and helped him stand. "You go on home and go to bed. Best to nip this in the bud before it gets any worse."

Joey started to protest, then thought better of it. The vertigo and nausea had passed, but the inexplicable anxiety remained. There was too much chance of injuring one of the delicate flowers in his care if he continued to try to work in this state.

"Yeah, okay." He tucked a stray curl behind his ear and gave Miranda a sheepish smile. "Sorry."

"Don't worry about it. We've all been there in the last few weeks. Guess it's finally your turn." She patted him on the back and picked up the watering can from the ground where it had fallen. "You need a ride? I can get one of the girls to take you home."

Joey considered. He felt vaguely feverish and shaky, but not really ill. The strange nervousness was the worst of it. "No, I can take the bus."

"Okay. Call me if you need anything."

"Sure thing." He gave her a wan smile. "Thanks."

"No problem. Just get yourself well before all my flowers die."

Joey laughed. "Bye, Miranda."

"Bye, hon."

Slipping out of his sturdy cloth apron, Joey hung it on the hook beside the door and went outside. The afternoon sun seemed brighter than usual, sending a lancing pain through his head. His skin felt tender and bruised.

Virus, he told himself, though he didn't believe it.

He caught the city bus at the corner a block from the nursery. Sinking into an empty seat, he leaned his head against the window as the city rumbled past outside. His body seemed to vibrate to some rhythm his conscious mind couldn't grasp. A maddening itch had begun between his shoulder blades, making him squirm.

What the fuck is happening to me? For the first time since the restlessness had come upon him a few weeks before, he felt afraid. Whatever was about to happen, he wished it would go ahead and happen. He wasn't used to being anxious and afraid, and he hated it.

Instead of getting off at his usual stop, Joey rode the bus all the way to the other end of University. He could walk to the Botanical Gardens bordering the college, then cut through the Gardens and across campus to reach his building. The longer walk, he figured, would calm him and help dispel the feeling of things crawling under his skin. He hadn't had any further episodes of dizziness or nausea since leaving the nursery. Surely he'd be okay to walk that far.

Within minutes, he regretted his decision. By the time he reached the entrance to the Botanical Gardens, alternating waves of heat and cold wracked his body and blurred his vision. The sounds of traffic and voices seemed muffled. His temples throbbed, and the itch in his back had increased to the point of pain.

At the entrance to the gardens, Joey tripped over a crack in the sidewalk and barely saved himself from a fall by grabbing a nearby bench. He clutched at it, head spinning. A shiver of unease ran up his spine. He'd never felt like this before. As if something were inside him, trying to burst out. It scared him.

After a few seconds, the dizziness passed. Joey let go of the bench and stood still for a moment. When he was sure he wouldn't fall, he staggered off down the path leading into the gardens.

The shade under the trees was hot and breathless. The air smelled of dry earth, ferns and dying flowers. Not a sound disturbed the unnatural stillness of the place. Joey almost thought he could hear the greenery shriveling.

Panic brushed at the edges of consciousness as he stumbled along the path. The strange whispering that had hovered in the back of his mind for days was stronger than ever, and half-formed visions flitted through his mind. If he focused on them, he knew what he would see—suffering. Dying. Fear. He thought he knew where it came from, and the implications filled him with a mix of terror and excitement.

Joey only realized he'd wandered off the path when he tripped over a tree root and went sprawling face down on the ground, hands splayed flat in the dirt. A barrage of unfiltered alien thought slammed into him, and he cried out.

Rain! his mind screamed, giving form and substance to the noise in his head. *Rain, we're dying, dying, save us!*

The sudden gloom and the patter of the first raindrops against the leaves wasn't surprising, considering that he'd felt it coming earlier, but the force of the drops was painful on his sensitized skin. As the patter became a steady, drenching rain, the bubble of pressure which had been building in Joey for weeks burst. His consciousness soared up and out, expanding to encompass what felt like every living thing for miles around. He felt the fierce pleasure of parched leaves and petals and roots as the cool water hit them, felt the thirst ease in the dirt beneath his cheek.

For the first time in far too long, the restlessness plaguing him faded away, leaving him calm and weak. Rolling onto his side, he curled into a ball, letting his exhaustion take him.

Just as his eyes closed, he noticed two things. First, the withered fern near his head appeared to be caressing his cheek with a newly green frond. Second, a lone firefly fluttered under the shelter of a nearby tree, a tiny warm glow in the dimness.

The pulse of blue light as his eyelids closed must be his imagination, he decided, and slipped into a dead sleep.

Chapter Two

Joey woke to the steady drum of rain on a roof. He smiled with his eyes still shut and burrowed deeper into the pile of pillows and soft sheets surrounding him. The formless anxiety he'd fought for so long was gone. He felt warm, safe and content. The headache he'd had earlier had vanished, along with the nausea and dizziness. In fact, he felt better than he had in years. Strong and invigorated, as if he could do anything. Even the weird voices in his head had faded to a vague susurration at the edge of consciousness.

Maybe I don't have that virus after all.

Oh. Wait...

The memories came back in a rush. The sensation of something momentous about to happen, leaving work and getting off the bus early to walk off his restlessness.

Falling in the woods. A flood of alien thought, a plea shouted silently to the sky not *by* him, but *through* him. The rain coming as if in response to that plea.

The firefly.

Joey sat bolt upright in bed, eyes flying open. He was in an unfamiliar room dominated by the huge bed in which he lay. Bedding in shades of green and cream covered the thick mattress. To his right, green curtains waved in the cool, damp breeze from the open window. Outside, it was dark. On the other side of the room, a kerosene lantern sat on top of a plain wooden dresser, bathing the room in a warm golden light.

A faint squeak of hinges sounded to Joey's left. He turned just in time to see a man he didn't know push the door open and step through. The stranger was tall, slender and graceful, with a long blond braid hanging over one shoulder. He wore a green T-shirt and a pair of faded jeans that hugged his willowy body just right. His bare feet made not a sound on the wood floor. The man's pleasant face broke into a dimpled smile when he saw Joey.

"You're awake," the man said, the musical lilt in his voice proclaiming his Irish background and making Joey's heart thud with a shock of recognition. "Did you sleep well?"

Joey stared, trembling all over. The voice was straight out of his memory. And those eyes...eyes that had haunted his dreams for twenty years. "Oh my God. It's you. You found me."

The man—*no, the faery*—blinked. "You remember, then?"

"Remember? I've been waiting my whole life for you to come back." A laugh bubbled up from Joey's chest at the thunderstruck expression on the faery's face. "God, I have so many questions."

The faery perched on the edge of the bed, silver-gray gaze fixed on Joey's face. "Ask, then, and I'll answer as best I can."

Kicking free of the tangle of sheets and pillows, Joey scooted closer and sat cross-legged with his bare knee pressed to the faery's denim-clad thigh. Joey noticed for the first time that his clothes had been removed and he was now naked, but the faery didn't seem to mind so Joey elected not to worry about it. "First things first. What's your name?"

"Braeden Shay, at your service." The faery bobbed his head in a slight bow.

Braeden's voice brushed Joey's skin like cashmere, making his stomach flutter. Joey licked his lips. "Where are we? And how'd you get me here? Last thing I remember is passing out in the Botanical Gardens."

"We're deep in the heart of the Shining Rock Wilderness, in the Smoky Mountains not far from your home." Twisting to face the window, Braeden waved a long, elegant hand toward the darkness beyond. "This cabin is glamoured to look like a bramble patch and is covered with repelling charms. The few hardy souls who hike this far will not bother us. Will not even notice us, I should think. I brought you here using the Space between worlds. Dangerous, that, but the alternative was worse."

"I don't have a fucking clue what you just said," Joey murmured. "Except the part about glamours and spells,

I've read all about those. And the part about where we are. I've hiked Shining Rock before." He leaned close enough to feel Braeden's heat. "How'd you find me?"

"I kissed you." Lifting a hand, Braeden rubbed a thumb across Joey's forehead. "Do you remember?"

A kiss as tender as his mother's pressed to his brow. Words he didn't understand whispered against his skin. "I'll come back for you, when you're ready."

Joey nodded. "I felt it tingling for days after."

"I spoke a spell to bind us through that kiss. It is old and powerful magic, allowing me to watch over you all your life without interfering until you needed me." Braeden's fingers trailed down Joey's cheek in a gentle caress. His silver eyes shone in the lantern-glow. "When you needed me, I knew, and I came to you."

A lump rose in Joey's throat. "What's happening to me, Braeden? I've been feeling so strange, for weeks now. And then that...whatever it was, happened in the gardens, and...and I don't know. I feel good right now, amazing in fact, but I still don't feel like me. I feel...different. I can't explain it."

Braeden's mouth curved into a wistful smile. "You're changing, Joseph. You do not yet realize how much. There's so much I need to explain to you. So much you need to know. That is why I've brought you here. This is a protected place. With any luck, we will not be found for quite a while. You'll have time to learn about your heritage, and what it means for your future and possibly the future of Tir-na-nog, the faery kingdom. And you will be able to learn to harness your powers."

Joey shook his head, puzzled and a little frightened by the things Braeden was saying. "I don't understand. I'm just a regular guy. The only thing special about me is you. You visiting me when I was little, and finding me again."

"You are special, Joseph." Braeden stroked Joey's hair, running his fingers through the tangled strands. "That's why I came to you when you were small, and that's why I am here now. Because you are unique in all the worlds, and it is my duty—and my privilege—to help you, and to protect you."

Joey should've been afraid, he knew. Clearly, his life had just been turned inside out in ways he couldn't yet comprehend. He should be scared and angry, demanding answers.

He should be. But he wasn't. At that moment, all he could feel was Braeden's hand in his hair, and a desire like he'd never known before flowing like lava through his veins.

It didn't surprise him. Somehow, he'd always known it would be this way.

Moving closer to Braeden, Joey lifted Braeden's free hand and kissed his palm. "Take the glamour off?"

Braeden let out a startled noise. "It's not safe to remove the glamour from this place. He has spies everywhere."

"Not the cabin," Joey clarified, putting the question of who "he" was aside for later. "You. Take the glamour off yourself. I want to see the real you."

"Are you certain?" Braeden's voice was a hoarse whisper. "Humans are often frightened by the way we look."

"I remember what you look like." Flowing white hair, porcelain-pale skin, a face like an angel. Wings towering to the ceiling and brushing the floor. After twenty years, the memory had lost none of its power, and every cell in Joey's body burned for it to be real once more. He took Braeden's hand, lacing their fingers together. "Please, Braeden."

Braeden's lips parted, a soft sigh escaping. Without a word, he pulled his hand from Joey's and stood. For a second, Braeden's form seemed to shimmer. Joey blinked, and the glamour Braeden had used to clothe and disguise himself was gone. The creature from Joey's childhood stood there, naked, white and shining, so beautiful he stole Joey's breath. The wings Joey had done his best to reproduce in ink rose above Braeden's head, the edges gilded with lantern light.

"Wow." Joey rose to his feet, drinking in the sight of the real Braeden. He was afraid to look away for fear the vision might vanish. "Just like I remembered."

Braeden laughed, the sound bell-like and nervous. "Is that good or bad?"

"Definitely good." The urge to touch moved his hands, and he didn't resist. Stepping closer, Joey laid his palms flat on Braeden's chest. An electric tingle ran up his arms at the contact. "Braeden?"

"Yes?"

Was it his imagination, or did Braeden's voice sound rough and breathless? Joey licked his lips. "Can I kiss you?"

Braeden sucked in a sharp breath. A faint but visible tremor ran through him. "Do you truly wish to?"

Nodding, Joey ran his hands up to caress the arch of Braeden's collarbones. "Yeah, I do. It's weird, you know, I'm not usually into getting physical with somebody I just met. But I'm just…" Joey broke off, fumbling for the words to describe the sudden, irresistible pull of desire for Braeden. It was like gravity, consuming and inescapable. "I'm drawn to you," he admitted finally, holding Braeden's gaze with his. "I can't fight it. I don't want to fight it."

Braeden laid his hands on Joey's cheeks and pinned him with an intense, searching look which made Joey feel far more naked than his lack of clothes. The silvery eyes brimmed with the same need Joey felt, underscored with a hint of sadness. Joey wanted to ask why Braeden was sad, but he couldn't seem to make the words come out. The feel of Braeden's hands on his skin utterly destroyed his power of speech.

Whatever Braeden was looking for in Joey's eyes, he must have found it, because he bent and pressed his lips to Joey's. In an instant, Joey's world spun off its axis and went flying, and he was lost. With a low moan, Joey wound an arm around Braeden's waist, opened his mouth and took the kiss deep.

He'd thought about it, of course, ever since he'd first become aware of his sexuality. Imagined what it might be like to hold the faery's bare body, to feel the electrifying touch of Braeden's lips on his. But even his most fevered fantasies had never come close to the reality of Braeden's slim but strong arms around him, or the mouth that took his with such hunger. Braeden's tongue tasted smooth and sweet, and his long fingers left tingling trails across Joey's bare skin.

As the kiss grew more heated, Joey felt a ghostly caress against his shoulders and calves and realized with a shock of delight that Braeden had wrapped his wings around him. The delicate membranous feel of them against his skin made him weak with desire. Wishing his own wings were alive instead of a tattooed image, he wormed a hand between their bodies and curled his fingers around Braeden's cock, gently manipulating the foreskin with his thumb.

"Sweet Goddess," Braeden gasped, his lips still brushing Joey's. "I have wanted you for years. I never dared dream this could happen."

Joey let out a breathless laugh. He stroked one of Braeden's wings with his free hand, and it undulated under his touch, sending a delicious shiver up his spine. "Please tell me you weren't perving on me when I was five."

The horrified expression on Braeden's face was answer enough. "By Danu, no. You were a singular child, to be sure, but I never felt this...this desire for you until you were a man full-grown." Digging his hands into Joey's buttocks, Braeden pulled him closer, pressing their erections together. "But by the Goddess, I do desire you now."

Joey moaned when Braeden's lips brushed the shell of his ear. Turning his head, Joey captured Braeden's mouth in another hungry kiss.

One step backward was all it took for Joey to tumble them both to the bed. He landed flat on his back with Braeden on top of him, straddling his hips. Braeden rubbed his cock against Joey's, sending sparks zinging over Joey's skin.

"Braeden," Joey growled, nipping Braeden's lip. "Can...can we...? I mean, you know, since you're—ah, oh fuck yeah—you're Sidhe and I'm human." Hooking a leg around Braeden's back, Joey canted his hips up, searching for more of Braeden's skin on his. "It's possible, right?"

Braeden drew back, staring hard into Joey's eyes. "There is nothing to stop us from making love. But, Joseph, I must tell you—"

Joey stopped Braeden's words with a hand against his lips. He didn't know what Braeden was about to say, but he knew whatever it was, he wasn't ready to hear it. "Don't. Not yet."

A faint smile curved Braeden's mouth. Leaning down, he gently kissed Joey's lips. "Love me, Joseph. Fill me like I've dreamed you would."

Something about Braeden's lyrical, old-fashioned way of speaking tugged at Joey's heart. He tucked a lock of gleaming white hair behind Braeden's ear. Which, he noted with a smile, was ever-so-slightly pointed at the tip. "Do you have lube and condoms?"

Braeden's brows drew together, his eyes fluttering closed. Joey felt a strange vibration in the air, followed by a faint popping sensation beside his right shoulder. Turning toward the almost-sound, he was surprised to see a small, unmarked blue vial. It hadn't been there a moment ago. He picked it up and examined it.

"Oil," Braeden explained. "We do not need condoms. We're not susceptible to human diseases, and the few illnesses our kind *do* succumb to cannot be stopped by a bit of latex."

We. Joey suppressed the rush of mingled terror and anticipation from that one word. He didn't want to think about that now. Not with Braeden kneeling astride his thighs, savagely beautiful and thrumming with a power Joey felt deep in his bones.

Flipping open the lid of the little vial, Joey poured a dollop of oil into his palm. A scent like rain and clover filled the room as he massaged the viscous fluid between his fingers. He pushed up on one elbow and reached a slippery hand between Braeden's legs.

Braeden let out a soft "oh" when Joey's slick finger rubbed against his entrance. His wings fluttered in response to Joey's touch. "Yes, Joseph. In me."

Panting, Joey circled the tiny opening, marveling at the downy softness of the skin there, the way the muscles rippled and relaxed as he stroked them. When the tightness eased suddenly and Joey's finger slipped inside, he and Braeden both gasped out loud. Joey's heartbeat faltered, stumbled and resumed in triple time.

"Fuck, you're tight," Joey breathed, staring up at Braeden with naked wonder. He pumped his finger a few times, just to watch Braeden's ghostly skin flush with lust. "How long since you've done this?"

Braeden moaned, translucent wings fanning the air behind him. He gave Joey a dazed smile. "Since before you were born."

"Damn." Pulling his finger out, Joey grabbed the vial again and poured more oil in his hand, then replaced the single digit with two. "Are you sure about this?"

Braeden nodded, sending a cascade of fine snowy hair tumbling over his shoulders to pool on Joey's stomach. "I need this. Need you."

He needs me. The knowledge glowed like an ember in Joey's chest, warming him to the core. Plunging his fingers deeper, Joey twisted until his knuckle brushed a small, firm spot almost at the limit of his reach. Braeden let out a keening cry, hips canting forward. A glistening drop of pre-come oozed from the tip of his cock and splashed onto Joey's belly, and Joey grinned. *I guess faeries have the magic button too.*

"Joseph, please," Braeden begged. "Please take me now."

The raw need in Braeden's voice shot through Joey's blood like lightning. Slicking his cock with the oil still coating his hand, Joey held his prick upright and pressed his free hand to Braeden's hip. Braeden straightened up and scooted forward on his knees, lining himself up with Joey's erection. Their gazes locked as Braeden sank down, taking Joey deep with one slow, smooth movement, and it was all Joey could do to keep from coming right then.

"Ah," Braeden gasped, head falling back so that his hair tickled Joey's thighs. His wings curled and straightened, the lantern light glowing through them. "Yes. Good."

Massive understatement, Joey thought, wishing he could say it aloud. He couldn't seem to get out anything but the grunts and moans ripped from him with every thrust into Braeden's body. Joey was hardly a blushing virgin, but sex had never felt like this before. Like he and his lover were connected by more than their joined bodies. The air around them crackled with the power of it.

Leaning forward, Braeden planted his hands on either side of Joey's shoulders. His wings curved to create a shimmering cocoon around them. Joey wrapped one hand around Braeden's cock, tangled the other into the long white hair falling over his shoulder and pulled him down into a devouring kiss. Braeden moaned into his mouth, thighs tightening around Joey's hips.

Outside, the rain made a staccato music to accompany the languid rhythm of their lovemaking. As the passion built between them and their movements became harder and more demanding, the wind rose and thunder rumbled over the night-shrouded mountains.

Just as Joey felt himself reach the point of no return, a brilliant flash lit the room. Braeden reared up, back arching. The white-hot flare of light caught in Braeden's wings and set his sweat-slick skin aglow. His eyes shone like a cat's, and his hair flew around his face in the moist breeze from the window. He looked wild and feral, like a child of the elements, and the sight was all it took to send Joey over the edge. Joey came with a shout barely audible through the crash of thunder, his body bowing with the force of his orgasm.

Braeden went perfectly still, eyes wide. *"A chuisle mo chroí,"* he whispered, and came in a hot sticky rush, shaking all over.

Pulling out of Braeden's body, Joey wiped his hand on the sheet then gathered Braeden into his arms and held him as the aftershocks of orgasm faded and died. Braeden's wings felt warm and alive under Joey's fingers, and his heartbeat galloped against Joey's ribs. Joey closed his eyes and breathed in Braeden's sunshine-and-grass scent mingled with the musk of sex.

It was several minutes before Joey became aware of the slithering noise coming from the window. The hairs on his arms stood up, his body going tense. A faint, sibilant hiss wormed its way into his brain. It felt familiar. *Just like before,* Joey realized in a burst of insight. *Just like in the Gardens.*

As if reading Joey's thoughts, Braeden lifted his head and kissed Joey's nose. "Do you hear?"

"Yeah. What is it?"

"Nothing to fear." Braeden smiled. "Look."

Joey turned his head. A long green vine covered with sweet-smelling honeysuckle blossoms spilled through the window. As Joey watched, it crept down the last few inches of wall and began extending itself along the floor toward the bed. It was like watching months of growth happen in a few seconds. Joey stared, fascinated.

"It wants to be near you, Joseph," Braeden said softly, brushing the tangled hair away from Joey's face. "It is drawn to you, as are all beings in the plant kingdom. This is your gift. I suspected all along, but I wasn't certain until the incident in the Gardens."

"Why doesn't this scare me?" Joey wondered, unsure if he was asking himself or Braeden. "For that matter, why doesn't it even surprise me?"

"Because you knew it in your heart all along."

Joey nodded, his gaze still fixed on the impossible movement of the vine. "I have some sort of power over plants, don't I?"

"Yes, you do. All green and growing things will come to your call." Dipping his head, Braeden kissed the corner of Joey's jaw. "This is powerful elemental magic. It's like electricity—a blessing if harnessed and controlled, but deadly if allowed to run wild. You must learn to control it. Part of my reason for being with you now is to help you do that. This particular form of magic is rare, and I myself am not gifted with it, but I will do everything in my power to help you learn how to use it."

Joey swallowed, his mind racing. The honeysuckle vine crept closer, new leaves sprouting before his eyes. "Why, Braeden? Why's this happening to me?"

"Because of what you are."

"And what's that?" Joey asked, though he thought he could guess.

Cupping Joey's chin in his palm, Braeden turned Joey to look at him. "The man who raised you was not your biological father. Your true sire is a lord of the Unseelie court."

"Oh, God," Joey breathed, feeling like he'd been punched. "So that means..."

"The blood of the Sidhe flows in your veins," Braeden confirmed. "You're half Fae."

Chapter Three

Joey lay underneath Braeden and stared up into his eyes, feeling stunned. If he were honest with himself, he'd have to admit a part of him had always known. But hearing it spoken out loud made it unbearably real.

"You said my...my f..." Joey stopped, took a deep breath and started over. "You said he was Unseelie. Does that mean I'm evil? I've read a lot about faery myths and legends over the years, only I guess they're not legends, really, are they? But most people say the Unseelie are evil. Christ, I don't want that."

"The stories humans tell about the Sidhe carry part of the truth, but not the whole of it. Much of what you think you know is false, and must be forgotten." Braeden soothed away Joey's budding panic with a kiss. "Human tales paint the Seelie court as good and the Unseelie as evil, but as with many such things, the reality is not so simple. The Unseelie court isn't inherently evil, merely amoral in a general sense. And whether one belongs to the Seelie or Unseelie court is an individual choice. Your sire's choice does not determine your own."

An ugly idea had taken root in Joey's mind. He wasn't sure he wanted to know, but he had to ask. "Before, you said someone was looking for us, and with any luck he wouldn't find us here for a while. Who were you talking about?"

Braeden's eyes darkened with a mix of sadness and empathy, and Joey knew he was right. "Your father," Braeden answered. "Lord Caratacus. He has desired your death since you were an infant."

"Oh." Joey turned to watch the vine now filling the window and sending more green tendrils across the floor. He tasted tears at the back of his throat. He'd never known any father other than Robert Vines, the man who'd raised him and loved him unconditionally his whole life. Nevertheless, it hurt to know his biological father not only hadn't wanted him, but was actively trying to kill him.

Gathering Joey into his arms, Braeden sat up and settled Joey onto his lap, wings folding around him. Joey slid an arm around Braeden's waist and laid his head on Braeden's shoulder, letting the silken touch of wings against his skin comfort him.

"I'm sorry, Joseph," Braeden whispered against his hair.

Joey swallowed, curling closer to Braeden's warmth. "Why does he want to kill me? What have I done?"

"You've done nothing, yet." Slender fingers stroked Joey's cheek. "But you will, one day. It is Caratacus's greatest fear, and Tir-na-nog's greatest hope."

"I don't understand." Lifting his head, Joey met Braeden's sympathetic gaze. "What am I going to do? And how does anyone know I'm going to do it?"

"Lord Caratacus murdered the Queen and took the throne by force while you were still in your mother's womb," Braeden answered, winding a strand of Joey's hair around one finger. "By the time you were born, he had all of Tir-na-nog under his control. The Fae are not above avarice, and he seduced many—particularly the Unseelie—with promises of power and wealth, thus creating an army of loyal brutes as wicked as himself. On the day of your birth, the court Seer made a prophecy. She said that Caratacus's firstborn—you—would one day take his life."

Joey stared into Braeden's eyes, shocked by what he'd just heard. "What? That's crazy! This is why he's after me now? This is why he's trying to kill me? Because of a stupid *prophecy?*"

"The future is not predestined, though those who attempt to change its course often bring about their own downfall." Braeden traced his fingers over the curve of Joey's shoulder. "In any case, Caratacus believes in both the prophecy and his own power to prevent it from happening. This is why he hunts you, and why he will not stop until he kills you, or dies himself in the attempt."

Closing his eyes, Joey rested his head in the bend of Braeden's neck. "You'd better tell me the whole story."

"Your mother was not the first to be seduced by one of the Sidhe and whisked away from her own world to the kingdom of the faeries. She did not love Caratacus. She hated and feared him, and all of the Fae, because Caratacus bespelled her and took her against her will. She fled Tir-na-nog on the night of your birth, for your life and her own, and brought you to the human world, where Caratacus couldn't find you. Those of us loyal to the Queen's son and heir to the throne helped her escape, but she wanted nothing to do with us." Braeden sighed. "Such a beautiful, spirited lass she was. So very strong. All she ever wanted was for the both of you to live your lives in peace. I only wish it could be that way."

Joey blinked away the tears stinging his eyes. "How did you find me when my f... When Caratacus couldn't?"

"I laid a spell on your mother when she left that allowed me to find her. Still, it took me five years to track her down." Braeden let out a soft, bitter laugh. "I am both a warrior and a spy, Joseph. I did what had to be done. When you were a child, Caratacus could not find you because your Sidhe half lay dormant. You were just another human in an endless sea of them. But we knew when your powers matured he would feel the surge of magic, and he would murder you before you could learn of his plans and flee him. So I found you, I bound you to me, and I remained in the world of humans so that when your Sidhe magic first manifested, I could find you before Caratacus."

Joey gaped. "You stayed here? You mean you haven't been back to your home in twenty years? Not even once?"

"No. It was too dangerous, for both of us." The corners of Braeden's mouth lifted in a wistful smile. "What is twenty years when you have all the vastness of time before you?"

Stunned, Joey shook his head. "So you really are immortal? Those parts of the stories are right?"

"Yes, they are. As are the claims that time flows differently in Tir-na-nog. When eventually I return to my home, I may find that only a day has passed, or I may find a century gone."

"And you were willing to take that risk?"

Braeden brushed his thumb over Joey's lower lip. "No matter how many years have gone by when I return, those who are dear to me will likely remain. Change happens there slowly, if at all. My risk in this was small."

It made sense. Still, it amazed Joey that Braeden had deliberately chosen exile in order to watch over him. Unable to find the words to express how he felt, Joey cradled Braeden's cheek in his palm and kissed him, letting all his wonder and gratitude flow through the connection of lips and tongues.

A cool, leafy touch on his thigh made Joey squeal in surprise. Breaking the kiss, he smiled at the honeysuckle vine attempting to wind around his leg. "I forgot all about this little guy."

Braeden laughed. "Focus your thoughts and ask it to go back outside."

"Do I have to?" Lifting a hand, Joey examined the green tendril curling around one finger. "I really don't mind it being in here, you know. I love plants. It won't hurt either of us, will it?"

"Most likely not. But it is a wild thing, and should thus be treated with caution." Braeden stroked a finger down the slender vine where it lay across Joey's leg. "You have elemental earth magic within you, Joseph. Asking this little one to do your bidding can be your first attempt at deliberately using that magic."

"Okay. I'll try." Concentrating as hard as he could, Joey found the thread of the vine's strange semi-sentient consciousness and touched his mind to it.

Instantly, he felt the vine's awareness of him, the stillness at the center of it as it awaited his command. Ignoring the urge to jump up and shout with sheer excitement, Joey let his mind form his request into terms a plant could understand. His gut told him he couldn't overthink it, or it wouldn't work, so he allowed his instincts to take over. With a speed that drew a startled yelp from Joey, the vine whipped away from his hand, across the floor and out the window.

Joey stared with his mouth open. "Shit, did you see that?"

"Indeed I did." Braeden beamed at him. "That was excellent, Joseph. It will be no work at all to teach you to control your powers."

"Cool." Yawning, Joey leaned against Braeden's chest. "Damn, I'm tired all of a sudden."

"It's not even been a full day since your powers came upon you. That alone would be exhausting, yet you've managed one demonstration of plant control and one brilliant round of lovemaking in addition to it." Planting a kiss on Joey's brow, Braeden lowered him to the mattress. "Sleep now, *a chuisle.* In the morning, we'll begin your training in earnest, and I'll answer any other questions you wish to ask."

Joey managed a sleepy smile as he snuggled into the pillows. "What does *a chuisle* mean?"

Joey's eyelids were already drifting closed, but he saw the tender shine in Braeden's eyes as he leaned down and kissed Joey's cheek. "It means 'my pulse'," Braeden told him, his breath warm and sweet against Joey's ear. "An old Gaelic endearment. Sleep now."

The bubble of happiness Braeden's words created in Joey's chest was almost enough to make him sit up, wind himself around Braeden and never let him go. But he was so tired, all his limbs limp and heavy, and he knew Braeden would still be there when he woke.

Joey sank into sleep with a smile on his lips and Braeden's long fingers caressing his face.

Braeden watched as Joseph's body relaxed into sleep. *So beautiful,* Braeden thought, running his fingers through the thick ebony waves spread across the sheets. Tresses that tumbled all the way to Joseph's waist when he stood. Asleep, Joseph looked innocent and untroubled, and so very young. Would he still look that way tomorrow? Or a week from now, or a year? Would he have any innocence left after all this was over?

Would he even survive the battle to come? The thought that he might not was unbearable.

A soft laugh escaped Braeden's lips. The one thing he'd never expected, when he chose this life of exile all those years ago, was to fall in love with his charge. It changed everything, and he wasn't sure if it would be Joseph's salvation or his undoing.

Braeden didn't know if the spell he'd cast had anything to do with his feelings for Joseph, but he supposed it didn't matter in the end. He loved Joseph, and there was no changing that.

Outside, the storm had passed, leaving only a faint drizzle behind. Rising to his feet, he paced over to the dresser and snuffed out the lantern. As the warm glow died, stars and moon peeked from behind the breaking clouds to cast a silver light across Joseph's sensual features. Fear squeezed Braeden's heart in a cold fist as he gazed at Joseph's sleeping face. Fear of the days and weeks to come, of what might happen to the man who'd become his whole world.

I cannot let Caratacus kill him. He must survive, and Caratacus must perish by his hand. Everything depends on it.

In order for Joseph to survive, and to ensure the survival of both the human and the Sidhe realms, Joseph had to shed his gentle nature and become a killer. And Braeden had to turn him into one.

No matter how many times he reminded himself of what was at stake, no matter how much he loved Joseph and wanted him to live, the knowledge that he must teach Joseph to kill never got any easier to bear.

Pulling the covers back, Braeden climbed into bed beside Joseph. He didn't feel the need for sleep yet, but the urge to hold and protect Joseph as he lay dreaming was too strong to fight. Curling one wing close to his body, Braeden turned onto his side and laid a hand on Joseph's belly. As if in response to Braeden's touch, Joseph rolled over and squirmed until his back was pressed against Braeden's chest. Braeden folded a wing around Joseph's body and buried his face in the man's shadowy hair.

Chapter Four

Joey surfaced slowly from sleep to the sound of leaves tossed in a strong wind. Blinking against the early morning sunshine, he opened his eyes and squinted out the window. Outside, birch and evergreen trees swayed against a sky of vivid, rainwashed blue. The breeze wafting in felt cool and damp against his face. Joey drew a deep breath, letting the fresh green scent soak into him.

Behind him, the mattress shifted, and Braeden's warm fingers traced the outline of Joey's tattooed wings. "Good morning, Joseph."

Braeden. My Sidhe lover. A grin spread across Joey's face. "Good morning."

"Did you sleep well?" The fingers trailed down Joey's back and over the curve of his buttocks.

"Like a rock." Yawning, Joey wriggled around to face Braeden, wrapped an arm around his neck and kissed him. "Mmmm. You're turning me on, touching me like that."

"I cannot help it." Braeden smiled. "You have wings."

For a second, Joey's heart leapt. Then he realized what Braeden was talking about. "Yeah. Matt's been working on them for ages. He just finished them last month."

A strange look darkened Braeden's eyes. "Matt? Who is Matt?" The wing not curled against Braeden's body quivered.

"The artist who did my tattoo." Joey grinned, stroking the agitated wing with gentle fingers. "What's the matter? Are you jealous?"

"No, of course not," Braeden said, the faint flush of his cheeks telling a different story. "I...I was simply asking."

"Uh-huh." Scooting closer, Joey slung a leg over Braeden's thighs. His morning erection brushed Braeden's cock, which instantly swelled at the touch. Braeden gasped. Joey gave a sharp thrust of his hips, wanting to draw that sweet sound from Braeden again. "Do you like it?"

"Like... Oh yes," Braeden sighed, his hand sliding down to cup Joey's ass.

"I meant my tattoo, actually." Leaning in, Joey flicked his tongue over the spot where the pulse fluttered in Braeden's white throat. "But this is nice too."

Moaning, Braeden sucked Joey's bottom lip into his mouth and let it go with a pop. "They are exactly like mine." He kissed Joey's chin, then the corner of his jaw. "Your wings, I mean. You...you are amazing, *a chuisle*."

Joey practically purred when Braeden's lips trailed feathery kisses down his throat. "Couldn't forget you." He arched his neck so Braeden could lap at the hollow just above his collarbone. "Always wanted to have wings like yours. So beautiful." Braeden's hand slipped between their bodies to cup Joey's balls, and he cried out. "Fuck, Braeden..."

"You certainly will. Later." A mischievous grin lit Braeden's face. "Right now, I want to watch you come by my hand. Is that all right?"

It's much more than all right, it's the best fucking idea I've heard in forever, Joey's mind screamed. What actually came out was a desperate whimper, but the surge of lust in Braeden's eyes said he got the point. Propping himself up on one elbow, Braeden took Joey's mouth in a searing kiss. His fingers curled around Joey's prick, stroking in a firm, fast rhythm.

Joey wished it could last for hours, but there was no way he'd be able to hold out more than a few minutes. The feel of Braeden's strong, sure fingers manipulating his cock was just too good. Braeden had a knee wedged between Joey's legs, holding them apart while the rocking of his hips rubbed his erection against Joey's thigh. Low moans spilled between Braeden's mouth and his as their mutual excitement grew.

Just as Joey's thighs began to tingle with the onset of orgasm, Braeden broke their kiss and skewered him with an intense silver-gray stare. He didn't say a word, but the depth of need in his eyes said it all. Joey came with eyes wide open and locked with Braeden's, feeling Braeden's release spill across his skin at the same time.

At that moment, he swore he could feel Braeden's heart beating in tandem with his own.

Letting go of Joey's cock, Braeden wrapped Joey in arms and wings and held him close, face buried in his neck. Joey stroked Braeden's hair, surprised and a bit concerned by the tension in Braeden's body.

"Braeden?" Joey rubbed his cheek against Braeden's. "Are you okay?"

Braeden nodded. "Yes," he answered, his voice muffled. "I'm fine."

"Then why are you so tense?" Lifting Braeden's chin, Joey searched his face for some clue to what was bothering him. Worry and regret shone from Braeden's eyes, and Joey frowned. "Braeden, what's wrong?"

Braeden sighed. "I wish I could take this task on myself and spare you from...from the things you'll have to endure."

A shiver of unease ran up Joey's spine. He thought he knew what Braeden was talking about. Last night, he'd been so stunned by the revelation of his true parentage and his real father's quest to kill him, he hadn't given much thought to the rest of the prophecy. The part that said he'd one day kill his own father.

The idea made him feel cold inside. Somehow, he knew that was what Braeden meant. That he would kill Caratacus himself if he could, to keep Joey from having to do it.

The implication that he would have to be the one to do the deed knotted Joey's insides with dread. He wanted to live, and he wanted Braeden to live. But he wasn't sure he had it in him to kill.

"Does it have to be me?" Joey twisted around to glance at the honeysuckle vine creeping across the windowsill, then turned back to Braeden. "Can't someone else kill him?"

"Many have attempted it. All have failed. Caratacus does not have great power on his own. But he has bound many of the Unseelie to him with the darkest of ancient blood magic, allowing him to draw on their powers at will, and giving enormous strength to himself and to those bound to him." Braeden traced the line of Joey's jaw with his fingers. "Only one of his own blood can overcome the dark magic and defeat him. You are the only one that remains. If you do not kill him, no one ever can."

"There aren't any, like, aunts and uncles, or cousins or something?" Jocy hated the pleading tone in his voice, but he couldn't seem to help it. "I can't be the only one left."

Sadness welled in Braeden's eyes. "He slaughtered his entire family years ago, right down to the remotest cousin. You are the only one still hidden from him."

"Oh." Joey frowned, his mind racing. "Well, so what happens if I don't kill him? Surely we can find a safe place somewhere. We can stay there, where he can't find us, and nobody has to die."

"There are many sanctuaries in this world. But we are not safe anywhere for long. Now that your magic has manifested, your blood calls to him." The edge of Braeden's wing caressed Joey's shoulder, the touch soft and soothing. "He cannot let you live. Even if you were to leave him be, the power he could gain by your death is a temptation he could not resist."

Joey shook his head. "I don't get it. How would he gain power by k...through my death?"

"You are half-human and half-fae. Half-breed children are rare, and their magic is unpredictable. Most do not survive to adulthood. Those who do tend to be incredibly powerful." Cupping Joey's face in his hands, Braeden held him with an intense, solemn gaze. "The raw power in you is enormous, Joseph. Greater than any I've ever encountered. And you are Caratacus's son. If your blood is spilled by his hand and he casts the proper spell at the moment of your death, the power he will gain will be enough for him to hold both the Sidhe and the human realms under his sway."

Joey stared into Braeden's eyes as the full horror of the scenario hit him. "That can't happen. We can't let it."

"No, *a chuisle*," Braeden agreed, stroking Joey's hair. "We can't."

A wave of pure panic washed over Joey, and he started to tremble. "I...I can't. Braeden, I can't, I can't kill anyone. I don't...I, I don't want to be a murderer. Braeden, please, don't make me, please don't." A sob tore from Joey's throat. "Braeden..."

Braeden's silver-gray eyes clouded with anguish. "Oh, Joseph. Come here."

Strong arms and satin-soft wings wrapped Joey in a comforting embrace. Winding his arms around Braeden's neck, Joey curled against him and let himself melt into Braeden.

He didn't cry, even though part of him wanted to. Instead, he buried his face in Braeden's neck and let the anger and fear wash through him unhindered. Once he stopped shaking, he felt calmer.

"Will you help me?" He kissed Braeden's throat and snuggled closer, trying to ignore the icy lump in his gut. "Will you teach me what I need to know?"

"That indeed is my purpose." Braeden's fingers trailed up and down Joey's spine, drawing shivers in their wake. "I am truly sorry, *a chuisle*. I would take this burden from you, if I could."

"I know." Drawing back a little, Joey raised his eyes to meet Braeden's. "Let's start right now. Before I lose my nerve."

To his relief, Braeden didn't argue. He smiled, graceful fingers twining through Joey's hair. "Very well. You may begin by practicing your control over plant life. Send our friend the honeysuckle vine back outside."

Joey blinked as he recognized the odd sensation of a plant's consciousness winding through his. He didn't have to look to know the vine was already climbing up the side of the bed. *Go back,* he thought to it, in the wordless images a plant could understand. *I'll call you when I need you, little one.*

The scratch and rustle of a vine rapidly retreating across a wooden floor sounded behind him, and he smiled. Whatever else the future had in store for him, there were some things he'd always have. This unexpected but exhilarating connection with the natural world was one. Braeden was the other.

It was enough.

♈

Joseph's blade opened a long red slash across Braeden's bare stomach, the force of the blow sending him staggering backward through the thick green grass of the meadow outside the cabin. Forcing himself not to wince at the sharp sting, Braeden beamed in pride.

"Excellent," he exclaimed, cleaning the blood from his swiftly knitting skin with a thought. His clothes were part of the glamour he always wore when not inside the cabin, so the blood faded from them as soon as it hit. "You're getting better."

Joseph gazed at him with wide, solemn eyes, fingers plucking at the thin workout pants Braeden had conjured for him. "Are you okay?"

"I am fine." Shaking his head, Braeden closed the distance between them and planted a kiss on Joseph's sweat-dewed brow. "I've told you many times, Joseph. The weapons you're training with are silver. Only a blade of iron can harm one of the Sidhe." He took Joseph's free hand and pressed the palm to the place where Joseph had cut him moments before. "Feel my skin. It's nearly healed already."

Joseph nodded, his face slightly pale but exhibiting none of the sheer horror it had the first time he'd cut Braeden while learning to use the knife. "Yeah, I know." Sighing, Joseph brushed a strand of windblown hair out of his eyes and dug one bare toe into the grass at his feet. "I'm sorry. This whole thing is just a lot to get used to, you know? I have trouble getting my head around it all sometimes."

"I know." Lifting Joseph's chin, Braeden brushed a kiss across his lips. "We can stop for a bit, if you like. We've been sparring most of the morning."

Joseph let out a sharp laugh. "I'd fucking love to stop. I'm tired, I'm filthy, and I stink. But we're not stopping until I get through your guard at least once."

"You cut me just now," Braeden reminded him.

"Yeah, 'cause you let me."

"I most certainly did not."

"You did." Grinning, Joseph backed up and pointed the long silver knife at Braeden. "Just because you're getting laid on a regular basis is no reason to go easy on me."

The fact that Joseph could joke about their situation eased some of Braeden's worry. So much rested on Joseph's shoulders. So many changes had been thrust on him in such a short time. He'd endured it all remarkably well, but the situation had taken a definite toll on him.

At first, Joseph had been nearly immobilized by fear and worry—fear for his own life and Braeden's, worry over how his abrupt disappearance would affect the people he loved. Going back to Asheville was not an option. Caratacus would already have spies there, waiting for Joseph's return. Joseph understood that. He hadn't mourned the loss of his possessions—though he'd worried about his plants—but being unable to contact those important to him had been a terrible blow. He'd hurled some shocking insults at Braeden when told he couldn't get in touch with his employer, his friends or even his mother. Braeden had stood silent during Joseph's tirade, then held him when he broke down and sobbed like a child. After the storm passed, a quiet and rather grim Joseph emerged and threw himself with savage determination into weapons training and feeling his way through his magical capabilities.

Joseph had advanced by leaps and bounds in the past two weeks. Already fit, his body had gone from nicely toned to beautifully sculpted, and his reflexes had become fast enough to border on precognition. He had a rather surprising aptitude for hand-to-hand combat, and the extent of his ability to control the local plant life was nothing short of astounding. Every time Joseph called the friendly little honeysuckle vine to him, or cleared a path through the forest with no more than a thought, Braeden was struck by a feeling of falling backward in time, to the long-lost era of gods and goddesses. Wandering naked through the forest, his long dark hair floating in the breeze to reveal glimpses of the tattooed wings, Joseph resembled a young godling of the wild woods. Only his expression, mournful and pensive, had ruined the illusion.

Braeden had missed Joseph's sunny smile these past days. It was good to see it return.

Braeden assumed a defensive pose, his knife held loosely in his palm. "Come, then. Show me what you've learned about hand-to-hand combat this fortnight."

"Okay." Joseph drew a deep breath and let it out, his body visibly relaxing. He dropped into a neutral stance, his grip on the knife a bit too tight but vastly improved from the first time he'd tried. "Ready."

Braeden paced sideways, keeping a critical eye on Joseph's technique as the man searched for an opening in Braeden's defense. The grass felt cool and prickly under Braeden's bare feet. He glanced around, making sure the little field remained empty other than himself and Joseph. A stone's throw to his right, the meadow sloped steeply downward. Puffs of white cloud drifted across an azure sky, and the Smoky Mountains rose in verdant waves all the way to the hazy horizon. To his left, the cabin lay between two outflung arms of birch and evergreen, hidden in a web of charms and glamours.

Nothing stirred but birds and insects, and the warm fragrant breeze. Nevertheless, Braeden couldn't seem to shake the feeling of something creeping up on him. It had niggled at his mind all morning and was becoming too insistent to ignore.

Joseph's knife hand fell to his side, and he cocked his head sideways with a frown. "Hey, Braeden?"

"Yes?" Dropping his defense posture, Braeden moved closer to Joseph. "You feel something, don't you?"

Joseph nodded. His gaze darted from side to side, eyes slightly too wide. "Something's not right. The plants' energy is disturbed." A frown creased Joseph's brow. "Whatever it is, it seems to be focused near the cabin."

Adrenaline shot through Braeden's veins. Trotting over to where the weapons case sat on the ground, he crouched beside it and flung it open. "Joseph, bring me your knife."

"What's wrong?" Joseph asked, jogging over and handing Braeden his silver knife.

"Perhaps nothing." Braeden placed Joseph's knife in the case alongside his own. "Perhaps everything."

"What the fuck's that supposed to mean?" Joseph demanded as Braeden took two heavy iron blades from the case. "Why are you getting out the iron weapons?"

"Because I'd rather be ready for no reason than to be caught unprepared." Braeden held out one of the knives, ignoring the faint burn of bare iron against his skin. "Take this."

Joseph closed his hand around the handle, staring at it like it might bite him. "What about you? Can you use an iron knife?"

"Touching it for a moment won't harm me, but I use one with a silver handle for combat." Lifting the ancient weapon from the foam padding, Braeden held it out for Joseph to see. "It was made for my grandsire by an artisan of Cleopatra's court."

Joseph's eyes saucered. He leveled a curious look at Braeden, but said nothing. Braeden was relieved. Now was not the time for Joseph to attempt to come to terms with the fact that centuries, not years, separated them.

"Let's go back to the cabin," Braeden said, rising to his feet. "If they attack us there, the spells I've set will warn us and give us enough time to escape."

Joseph nodded. His face was grayish underneath the caramel skin tone, but his hand gripped the knife handle without shaking, and his eyes were clear.

Smiling, Braeden laid a hand on his lover's cheek. "Only a fortnight, and already you face danger without panic. You have the soul of a warrior, *a chuisle*."

A charming blush rose in Joseph's cheeks. Eyes shining, he tilted his head up and kissed Braeden, a swift brush of lips that was over too quickly.

The small touch made Braeden's tightly furled wings vibrate against the bonds of the glamour he wore while outside the cabin. *By Danu, he needs no magic but his kiss to hold me captive.* In the past two weeks, Braeden had memorized every inch of Joseph's body. He'd learned Joseph's taste and smell and the texture of his skin so well he was sure he could pick his lover out from a crowd of hundreds while blindfolded. But nothing intoxicated him like the man's kiss. It was an addiction he never wanted to cure.

"Come," Braeden said, taking Joseph's free hand and silently charming the weapons case to float behind them. "Let's get inside."

Joseph kept close to Braeden's side as they walked the short distance to the cabin. "They're here, aren't they?" He gripped Braeden's hand tight. "Caratacus's people. They've come for me."

"Possibly." He gave Joseph's fingers a squeeze. "But they can't imagine how strong you've already become. And I will die before I let them have you."

Joseph's gaze locked onto Braeden's face. His deep brown eyes brimmed with naked apprehension. "I don't want you to die for me, Braeden."

"Believe me, I have no intention of letting either of us die if I can help it." Under the shade of a gnarled old birch whose branches spread over the cabin roof, Braeden stopped and glanced toward the cabin. "If Caratacus has indeed found us, *a chuisle,* it will be the beginning of a dangerous time. You're not yet ready to face him down, but he will perceive that your powers are being honed very rapidly indeed, and therefore his pursuit will be relentless. We must both keep our eyes and ears open at all times, and our magic at the ready."

"I understand." Joseph tilted his head back, staring into the greenery above them. "I wonder if..."

His voice trailed off, but his lips continued to move. With a creak and a rustle, one of the low-hanging birch branches bent and curved around Braeden's chest. A sharp thrill coursed through him, and he smiled. Joseph's control over his magic had become strong indeed if he could bend a tree as old as this one to his will.

"Caratacus would do well to fear you, Joseph." Lifting their still-joined hands, Braeden kissed Joseph's fingers. "Let us go inside now. We are too exposed out here."

"Okay."

Without so much as a word or a look from Joseph, the branch withdrew. Braeden eyed it as they stepped up to the cabin door. Even though he himself had no power over plant life, he had an affinity with all things in the natural world, and he could feel the tree's watchfulness.

Joseph has instructed it to guard the door, and it is doing his bidding.

It was an impressive feat, especially for one whose powers had only just manifested, and who had barely begun to learn how to use them. The honeysuckle vine outside the bedroom window was one thing—young and curious, as eager and malleable as a puppy. This tree was another thing entirely. Ancient as the mountains themselves, wild and proud and untamable. A being such as this one did not bow to anyone, yet it had allowed Joseph to command it.

Caratacus should fear him indeed.

Letting go of Joseph's hand, Braeden curled his fingers around the doorknob. "Let me go in first. Just in case the cabin is compromised."

Joseph's eyes widened and his shoulders tensed, but he remained calm. His knife hand came up, the weapon held in a steady grip. "I'm ready."

Braeden nodded, turned the knob and flung the door open, half expecting to see Caratacus himself standing in front of the fireplace.

The room was empty.

Behind him, Joseph let out a whooshing breath. "He's not here."

"No, it appears he isn't." Frowning, Braeden paced slowly across the room to the bedroom door, with Joseph at his heels. "But I fear he's found us, even though he cannot get into the cabin. Something feels wrong."

Joseph drew closer, the heat of his body radiating against Braeden's back. "Let's just get our stuff and leave, huh? You said there's other places we can go."

"Yes. That is precisely what we should do." Turning to glance at his lover, Braeden pushed the partly open bedroom door wide. "We'll glamour ourselves and travel by traditional means, if possible. It's safer than—"

"Fuck!" Joseph shoved Braeden aside just as a gray blur flew past his head, buried itself into the wood of the wall behind him, and resolved into a small but deadly iron blade with a silver handle.

Caratacus stood on the other side of the open bedroom door, long chestnut hair braided away from his face, virulent green eyes blazing with murderous fury. His wings, pure white veined with blood red, snapped back and forth. Naked, his pearly skin glowing with power, he was a terrifying sight. Four of his followers stood behind him in a row, faces blank and eyes glazed.

"Give him to me," Caratacus hissed, stalking forward and reaching a long, thin hand toward Joseph. "Give me my son."

Dropping the glamour he still wore, Braeden fanned his wings out to their full span and placed himself between Caratacus and Joseph. "You will not have him while I live."

Caratacus's thin lips curled into a cruel smile. "Then I will have him in short order."

Lifting a hand palm out before him, Caratacus muttered something below the range of Braeden's hearing. The four silent Sidhe stiffened, each raising an arm in perfect synchronization. Pain bloomed in Braeden's skull as the air around him grew thick and heavy.

Summoning his own magic, Braeden threw a protective shield around himself and Joseph. It wouldn't last long—the combination of Caratacus's own power and the powers of his followers was too much for him to fight for any length of time—but perhaps it would be enough.

He lifted his knife. A direct blow to Caratacus's heart wouldn't kill him, since the four bound to him by blood would no doubt remove the blade at once and use their magic to heal him. It would slow him down, however, and give Joseph and himself a chance to escape. But before Braeden could throw the knife, something green, slender and sweet-smelling whipped around Caratacus in a movement so fast Braeden's eyes couldn't follow it. The pressure in his head abruptly dissipated, and Braeden didn't waste another second.

Yanking Joseph into the crook of one arm, Braeden opened a portal into the Space between the worlds and whisked them both inside. Caratacus's angry bellow as he struggled against the honeysuckle vine was cut off with the closing of the portal behind them.

A heartbeat later, Braeden half-dragged Joseph through another portal and into a hidden hollow surrounded by jagged, snow-covered peaks. It was night here, on the other side of the world, and cold enough to freeze living tissue solid within seconds. Braeden cast a spell of protection against the cold, forming a bubble in which he and Joseph floated just above the pristine snow.

Joseph stared at him for a moment, brown eyes huge and haunted. Then he dropped his knife and fell into Braeden's arms. Lacking the power to do anything else, Braeden let his own knife fall, curled his wings around Joseph and held him until his trembling subsided.

Chapter Five

Joey stood before the window of the cabin Braeden had somehow created from snow and thin air, staring at the mountains looming against the sky and the moonlight reflecting off the unbroken snow on the ground. Outside, ominous gray clouds gathered while rising winds drew ribbons of snow from the rocky peaks. Inside, the fire Braeden had started crackled on the hearth and sent orange light dancing across the walls.

The blaze had quickly heated the air to a nearly tropical level, for which Joey was grateful. Whatever hell Braeden had taken him through between Shining Rock Wilderness and these icy mountains, it burned with a cold that penetrated him to the core and left him wondering if he'd ever be warm again.

The Space between the worlds, Braeden had called it. A blank, icy darkness with nothing to anchor the eye, or the mind. Joey wished he'd never have to visit the place again, but he knew it was a vain hope. They'd used that route to get to this spot, and from the looks of it, there was no other way out. Wherever they went after this, they'd have to travel once again through that horrible static-filled nothingness to get there.

He wasn't sure how long they'd been here, wherever "here" might be. Minutes, or hours, or days. Years, maybe. Time had stopped for Joey the second he'd locked gazes with his real father and seen the loathing and bloodlust in those green eyes.

Braeden had told him, and he'd believed it, but he hadn't really known. Now he did, and the knowledge nearly paralyzed him.

How can I do this? Joey mused, trailing a fingertip through the condensation fogging the window. *How can I possibly fight so much hate?* Closing his eyes, he covered his face with his hands.

The soft pad of bare feet across a wood floor sounded behind him, then Braeden's arms slid around his waist. "Joseph?" Braeden pressed himself against Joey's back and kissed his temple. "It's all right, *a chuisle.* We're safe, for now."

Joey let his hands drop and opened his eyes. Leaning against Braeden's chest, he rested his head on his lover's shoulder. Braeden's wings curved forward to cradle him, and he let himself relax into the embrace.

"We left your weapons case."

"We each have one weapon." Braeden kissed his hair. "The rest can remain where they are, for now."

"Where are we?" Joey asked, gently stroking the edge of Braeden's wing.

A soft pleasure sound escaped Braeden's lips, and Joey smiled. It hadn't taken him long to figure out how much Braeden loved it when he touched his wings.

"We are in Nepal, in the highest peaks of the Himalaya Mountains," Braeden answered, and kissed Joey's neck. "We'll only stay here long enough to throw Caratacus off track. He won't expect to find us here."

"Why not?"

"For the same reason I don't wish to remain here for long." Braeden nodded toward the gathering storm outside. "Nothing grows in this place. He'll expect us to surround ourselves with growing things, because of your power."

"Oh." The mention of Caratacus made him feel cold inside. Shivering, he pulled Braeden's arms tighter around him. "It'd be nice to have plants around. I got used to talking to them."

"What you did back there at the cabin was amazing," Braeden breathed against Joey's ear. "When we leave here, I'd like to go to South America." Sliding a hand between Joey's legs, Braeden cupped his balls through his pants. "There's a magical shelter in the Orinoco River basin. I prepared it many years ago, when you were just a child. I prepared many such places all over the world, but this one will suit our purposes perfectly."

A tremor of need ran through Joey's body as Braeden's thumb traced the outline of his shaft through the thin sweats. He moved his feet apart, letting his thighs open. "What...what purposes?"

"You have a rare power." Braeden slipped his hand inside Joey's pants. "And you already have greater control over that power than I've ever seen wielded." A fingertip rubbed firm circles on the sensitive skin behind Joey's balls. He moaned, arching into the touch. "This ability of yours is the key to defeating Caratacus." Dipping his head, Braeden mouthed the shell of Joey's ear. "The jungle is overflowing with green and growing life. It is there we must face him."

Groaning, Joey turned in Braeden's embrace, buried both hands in his hair and kissed him. "I don't want to think about that right now," he growled, pulling back so he could see Braeden's face. "Let's fuck."

Braeden's plump lips parted, his eyes darkening from silver to storm gray. "*A chuisle.* I have never desired anyone as I do you."

"I'll take that as a yes," Joey said, and dropped to his knees.

Once again, Joey thanked his lucky stars that faeries mostly went nude, using spells and glamours to cover and warm themselves when necessary. Or at least Braeden did, and he claimed most of his kind did the same. Wrapping a hand around Braeden's rapidly stiffening shaft, Joey peeled back the foreskin with his thumb and forefinger and licked the rosy, glistening tip.

"Oh sweet Goddess," Braeden gasped, burying his fingers in Joey's hair. "Joseph...you...your mouth is... Oh, oh, Joseph, yes..."

Smiling, Joey circled his tongue once more around the head of Braeden's prick, then pulled back to watch the pre-come ooze like diamond drops from the slit. "Your cock is so beautiful," he murmured, staring at the leaking organ in his hand. "I could just look at it for hours."

Braeden's laugh came out choked and breathless. "I hope you intend to do more than simply look, now that you've aroused my lust."

Joey stole a glance at Braeden's flushed and heavy-lidded face before turning his attention to his lover's erection. It was difficult not to lose himself in the sight of it—the thick, smooth shaft, pearly white skin blushing the barest pink, the faint iridescent shine of the head with the foreskin pulled back. This part of Braeden was as perfect in Joey's eyes as the rest of him. Ethereal, but strong. Exquisitely beautiful, yet utterly masculine, with a clean, earthy scent that made Joey's crotch throb and his mouth water.

Leaning forward, he parted his lips and breathed across the sensitive glans. Braeden trembled, his fingers clenching in Joey's hair. "Joseph, please. Please."

"Say it, Braeden." Tightening his grip on Braeden's shaft, Joey bent to tongue the testicles drawn snug against Braeden's body. "Tell me what you want."

A telltale hitch of breath and a pulse of blood through Braeden's cock told Joey exactly how excited Braeden was. Joey smiled. He'd been surprised and delighted to learn Braeden loved dirty talk during sex.

"Suck my cock," Braeden ordered, the words sounding shockingly sexy in his soft voice with that musical Irish accent. "Please, *a chuisle,* please, suck me."

Fuck, yes. Moving both hands around to clutch Braeden's ass, Joey opened wide and swallowed him down.

Sucking cock had always been one of Joey's favorite sexual acts, ever since he'd first tried it with his best friend in high school. He loved the sensation of a wide, hot shaft stretching his jaw open and filling his throat, the smell of sweat and excitement, the bitter-slick slide of semen down his throat. Even more, he loved turning a man into a quivering, begging mass, lost in a world of pure sensation. He could usually climax just from the headspinning rush that came from knowing the tiniest stroke of his tongue or hollowing of his cheeks held so much power.

Yes, he'd always loved sucking cock. But Braeden brought the experience to a whole new level. Everything about him was different. Better. More intense. The incredible softness of his skin, the faintly sweet taste of his semen, his scent which reminded Joey of high green grass in the sunshine. The way he babbled in Gaelic when Joey deep-throated him, wings fluttering against Joey's shoulders in a gossamer caress.

God, he loved the touch of those wings.

"Ah, Joseph," Braeden moaned, hips moving in tiny pulses. "Close. So close."

Joey pulled his mouth from Braeden's cock and stared up into his eyes. "Fuck my mouth, Braeden."

Braeden's eyes went hot, his wings undulating. Without a word, he grabbed the back of Joey's head and shoved his cock down his throat.

Relaxing his muscles to take Braeden in to the root, Joey rolled his eyes up until he could see Braeden's face. He loved watching Braeden in the throes of orgasm. Loved the slight tilt of his head, the quiver of his wings, the way his skin seemed to glow with an inner light. So beautiful.

And so very inhuman.

But then again, so am I.

The knowledge curled like a ribbon of ice in his belly, bringing with it a resentment which had grown stronger and uglier each day. Shoving the unwelcome feelings away, Joey pulled off of Braeden's prick long enough to slick a finger with saliva, then gulped Braeden down again and pushed the slippery digit deep into his ass.

"Joseph!" Braeden cried, and came with his cock buried in Joey's throat. His semen was warm and sweet, the liquid thinner but more copious than human come. Joey swallowed it down, keeping his gaze fixed on Braeden's face.

He's mine. Only mine. Forever.

How Joey could be so certain after such a short time, he had no idea, but he'd never been more sure of anything in his life. The simple truth of it gave him something to hang onto amidst the whirlwind of upheaval in his life, and he was grateful for that.

Braeden collapsed to his knees, his cock slipping from Joey's mouth with a pop. A dazed smile spread across his face. "I begin to believe your greatest magic lies in your lips and tongue." Framing Joey's face in his hands, he pressed a wet kiss to his mouth. "Once again, you have undone me, *a chuisle*."

Something warm and tight tugged at Joey's chest. Closing his eyes, he wound both arms around Braeden's waist and gave himself up to the kiss, opening wide for his lover's tongue. Braeden's hips rocked against his, pressing his prick between them and tearing a guttural moan from him. He felt Braeden's lips curve into a smile.

"My body is yours, Joseph," Braeden said, fingertips tracing the outline of Joey's tattoo. "Fuck me."

As always, hearing Braeden say those words sent lust spiking up Joey's spine. He wasn't sure why, exactly. It was a common enough phrase; he'd heard it before, and he'd said it himself from time to time. But something about the sound of those vulgar words from Braeden excited Joey almost unbearably. Maybe because Braeden normally didn't say such things. Joey certainly couldn't picture him saying it to anyone else.

Wishful thinking, the practical part of him warned.

The larger part of him—the part which had always operated on gut instinct—knew better.

"Lie down," Joey ordered, pushing on Braeden's shoulders. "God, you have no idea how much it turns me on that you're a bottom."

Braeden obediently stretched out on his back, pale brow furrowed. "A what?"

"A bottom." Joey grinned at him. "Means you take it up the ass."

"Oh." The rosy flush in Braeden's cheeks deepened. "You humans have the most...interesting phrases."

But I'm not human anymore.

With that thought, the bitterness Joey had been fighting for days rose inside him once again. He hated feeling that way, hated how it made him wish none of this had ever happened. It *had* happened, and no amount of wishing could change that. Besides, if none of this had happened, he never would've had Braeden in his life.

Keeping that knowledge in the forefront of his mind, Joey pushed Braeden's thighs apart, bent and kissed his knee. "Lube?"

The now-familiar blue vial of oil appeared on the floor beside them. Joey snatched it up, opened it and coated his fingers in fragrant slickness. Lifting Braeden's right leg, he plunged two fingers into his ass.

Braeden let loose a string of curses in Gaelic. He hooked his hands behind his knees, pulling his legs up and spreading them wide. "Joseph...*a chuisle.* Take me now."

Heat shot through Joey's veins as he gazed down at the incredible creature beneath him. He wanted to tell Braeden how gorgeous he looked naked, spread and writhing, wings beating a whisper-soft rhythm against the floor. But all the blood in Joey's body seemed to have collected in his cock, leaving him dry-mouthed and bereft of the words to express how he felt.

Luckily, he and Braeden had become well-versed in the language of each other's bodies.

Leaving his fingers buried inside Braeden, Joey leaned down, snagged one pink nipple between his teeth and tugged. Braeden gasped, back arching. His skin slid warm and damp against Joey's, and suddenly Joey couldn't wait a second longer. He pulled his fingers out of Braeden's ass and shoved his prick in.

"Oooh," Braeden moaned, legs winding around Joey's waist. "Yes, oh Goddess you feel amazing inside me."

Joey couldn't have answered if his life depended on it. He drew a few shallow breaths, shaking with the effort of holding still. If he moved, he'd come, and he didn't want to come yet. He wanted to revel in the living heat of Braeden's body as long as he could. Neither of them knew what lay in the immediate future. For all they knew, this could be the last time they made love.

If this was it—if this was their final time together—Joey wanted to make it last.

Joey leaned over and planted his hands on either side of Braeden's ribs, sliding his fingers carefully under Braeden's wings. His hair, which had long ago come loose from its braid, fell over his shoulders to enclose him and Braeden in a tangled curtain. He stared down into his lover's lust-glazed eyes, and the tenderness there clutched his chest in a hot fist.

Slipping a hand around the back of Joey's head, Braeden pulled him into a rough, wet kiss. Joey tilted his head, taking the kiss deeper, eating at Braeden's mouth like a starving man.

"Move," Braeden breathed, biting Joey's lip. "Fuck me."

Joey groaned, the undulation of Braeden's insides sending shivers racing along his skin. Bracing his knees on the floor, Joey pumped his hips as slowly as he could bear. "God. So fucking good, Braeden." Joey angled up to hit Braeden's gland, just to hear those low, sweet curses again. "Don't want this to end. Want it to last."

Braeden's eyes snapped into focus, his gaze locking with Joey's. "Forever, Joseph. Always." His tongue flicked out to capture a bead of sweat from Joey's upper lip. Long fingers caressed Joey's cheek and tangled in his hair. "*Tá tú go h-álainn. Táim i ngrá leat.*"

Joey didn't know what the words meant, but they sent his pulse racing and his spirit soaring. The hot glow in his belly spread up and out, until his skin burned with it. His body moved of its own accord, fucking Braeden harder, faster.

"Brae...Braeden...I can't... God, I need...I need..."

The words died in Joey's throat, but Braeden seemed to understand. "Let go, *a chuisle,*" he whispered, the words broken by the force of Joey's thrusts. "Give yourself to me."

As if in response to Braeden's gentle command, Joey's body jerked with a sudden wash of pleasure, making him gasp. His hips pistoned, driving himself deep into Braeden, over and over again, until the pleasure sharpened and intensified and culminated in a rush of pure blazing rapture. He came buried deep inside Braeden's body, wrapped in Braeden's arms and legs and wings, surrounded by Braeden's scent. The scent that had already come to mean home to him.

By the time the orgasm loosened its grip on him, Joey's arms had begun to shake. He rested his head in the curve of Braeden's neck, smiling at the way Braeden shivered when Joey's cock slipped out of him. Joey relaxed into Braeden's embrace, soothed by Braeden's graceful fingers in his hair.

They lay like that for a long time, holding each other in silence while the fire crackled and the wind keened outside. Bits of windblown ice peppered the window in rapid little clicks like tapping fingernails. Clouds and falling snow veiled the moon.

Watching the warm light of the fire flicker around the room, Joey had the feeling the rest of the world could disappear and he and Braeden would never know. The thought was both terrifying and oddly comforting.

Without warning, an image of Joey's mother popped into his head. He hadn't thought of her in a couple of days, caught up as he'd been in learning to control his powers instead of letting them control him. For the first time, it hit him that he might never see her again. A hard knot formed in his guts.

Braeden's long legs unwound from Joey's waist. "What are you thinking?" he asked, cheek rubbing against Joey's hair.

Joey swallowed. "Nothing."

Beneath him, Braeden's chest rose and fell in a soft sigh. "I can feel your sorrow, Joseph. Tell me what troubles you."

Lifting his head, Joey propped an elbow on Braeden's chest and rested his chin in his hand. "I was thinking of my mom," he said, watching Braeden's face. "I want to go see her."

Braeden's expression turned careful, the way it always did when he was about to say something he knew Joey wouldn't want to hear. "We've spoken of this before. You know we can't do that, and you know why."

"Yeah, I know it's dangerous. But this might be my last chance to see her." Joey flashed the smile that always melted Braeden. "She's bound to be worried about me. Can't I at least talk to her for a minute? Just to ease her mind?"

Shaking his head against the floor, Braeden touched Joey's cheek. "It's too dangerous, for her as much as for you. More so, perhaps."

Joey pushed off of Braeden's chest and jumped to his feet, trying not to give in to the anger rising in him. "What if I die, huh? What if Caratacus kills me and I never get to tell my mother goodbye, and that I love her? I want to see her, Braeden, please."

"I know," Braeden answered, rising to stand beside Joey. He laid a hand on Joey's cheek. "Believe me, *a chuisle,* I understand your desire to see your mother. But I cannot allow it. I'm truly sorry, Joseph."

Helpless fury turned Joey's vision red. Shoving Braeden's hand away, he stepped back and stood shaking just out of Braeden's reach. "How can you possibly understand what I'm feeling right now? You come barging into my life, telling me I have to kill my own father or he's going to kill me, you spend the last two weeks trying to turn me into a *murderer,* and you expect me to believe you understand anything at all?"

Hurt flashed through Braeden's eyes and was gone before Joey could properly register it. "I am not perfect, Joseph, but I am trying to do what's best for you, and for your mother."

"Fuck you!" Joey shouted, pointing an accusing finger at Braeden. "I didn't ask for any of this shit. I didn't want it. I don't want to be the fucking savior of the Faeries, I just want my fucking life back!"

For a second, the world went still. Joey blinked, stunned by what he'd just said. But he didn't take it back. Ugly as it was, it was still the truth.

Braeden crossed his arms, his gaze full of unwavering patience. When he spoke, his voice was gentle as ever. "Caratacus cares nothing for your mother. If you go to her, he will follow you, and if he cannot kill you right before her eyes he will take her and use her to bring you to him. And when she has served her purpose, she will die slowly in the dungeons beneath his castle. Would you risk that, just to see her once more?"

Bitterness flooded Joey's mind. Braeden was right. He knew it, and hated it. Shaking his head, Joey turned and stalked over to the window to stare out into the night. Storm-tossed snowflakes swirled in and out of the darkness, and the wind howled like a banshee. He liked it. The violent weather matched his mood.

Faint footfalls sounded behind him. He bit his tongue and forced himself to hold still. He was furious with Braeden, furious with life, furious with the whole world, and a little afraid of what he might be capable of if he didn't control himself.

"Joseph?" Braeden's hand brushed his shoulder. "Are you all right, *a chuisle*?"

Braeden's tentative touch, the sweet Gaelic endearment, and especially the sympathy in Braeden's voice, made Joey's blood boil. Spinning around, he pinned Braeden with a hot glare.

"No, I'm not fucking all right. In case you hadn't noticed, my whole fucking life is gone. Either I die, or I kill somebody else, and I *fucking hate that.* I hate it. I want to go back to being just me, without knives and powers and fucking psychotic faeries after me." Fisting both hands in his hair, Joey pulled until it hurt, trying without success to drown out the rage inside him. "Why'd you have to find me? Why couldn't you just leave me alone? I don't want to be a fucking murderer. I'd rather have let him kill me."

Anguish clouded Braeden's eyes, and Joey hated that worse than anything. He knew he should tell Braeden he was sorry, that he hadn't meant it, that he knew he had to kill Caratacus for the good of every soul in two worlds, that he was grateful to Braeden for saving his life, and even more so for becoming a part of it. But the anger and resentment he'd tried to ignore for two weeks had him in its grip, and he couldn't shake it. It was like watching a plane crash, horrified but unable to stop it from happening.

He opened his mouth to speak, and had no idea what was about to come out. But before he could say a word, Braeden closed the distance between them, grabbed his shoulders and shook him.

"Do you truly think you are the only one ever to walk a path they did not choose? I know you hate what has happened to you, Joseph, I know you hate..." Braeden's breath hitched, his voice breaking for a second, and the sound cut Joey to the core. "You hate me right now. But this situation is not of my making any more than it is of yours, and I cannot change it for you. No one can. I would give my life to give you back what you've lost, but I cannot. There is no going back, you must understand that."

Braeden's face was a stern mask, but Joey saw the pain hiding in his eyes. The fact that he'd hurt Braeden so badly just made Joey angrier. In that moment, he hated himself more than anything else.

A homesickness like he hadn't felt in years swallowed Joey in a wave of grief for his lost childhood. Squeezing his eyes shut, he shook off Braeden's grip and pressed both palms to his forehead. "Jesus *fuck,* I wish I could just go back home."

The words were barely out when Joey's body jerked backward into bottomless, icy cold. He opened his eyes just in time to catch a glimpse of Braeden reaching for him, eyes huge and face bleached whiter than ever with shock. Then the portal closed and Joey was falling through the screaming emptiness of the Space between the worlds.

He couldn't see, couldn't think, couldn't even breathe. Before he had time to panic, there was a sharp tug low in his spine. He tumbled out of midair and landed face down on the ground, with bright sunlight beating on his bare back.

Pushing himself to a sitting position, Joey looked around. He was in the middle of a dry, grassy field. The land was perfectly flat in every direction, the heat shimmer forming wavering mirages in the dirt. On the horizon, cars zipped back and forth on a road hidden by distance. Heat pressed down like a weight, damp and breathless.

Something about the place seemed familiar. Frowning, Joey twisted around to look behind him. About a hundred yards away lay a sparse growth of cypress trees which spread and thickened into a dense forest. Joey shaded his eyes with his hand and squinted, and suddenly knew what he was looking at.

His memories filled in what he couldn't see. Not far beyond those first trees, the land grew boggy and treacherous. Stagnant pools and slow-flowing streams twisted through the undergrowth. If you went far enough, you came out of the trees into a bare place where the ground looked solid but wasn't, and a curious little boy could sometimes find the bones of small animals caught in the thick brown mud. He'd lost more than one pair of sneakers there in those childhood adventures.

He was looking at Sawyer's Swamp, just a few miles from the house where he'd grown up.

He'd come home.

Joey stared, fighting panic. He'd wanted to come back here, of course he had, but not like this. Not with Braeden half a planet away where Joey couldn't see him, couldn't touch him or kiss him or feel those beautiful wings enclose him in silky living warmth.

Not when he'd said such terrible things, but hadn't said the one thing he should have. Not when he hadn't told Braeden how much he loved him.

"I'm sorry, Braeden. God, I'm so fucking sorry. I didn't... I didn't know I could... Fuck. Fuck."

Bowing his head, he covered his face with his hands and fought to get his emotions under control. Sitting in the field stewing in his regret wouldn't change things. He had to stay calm and think if he wanted to find a way back to Braeden. And he did, more than he'd ever wanted anything.

More than you want to see your mother again? a subversive corner of his mind prodded. *You're here. Go see her, talk to her. Braeden will probably come here to find you. He's smart, he'll know this is where you went, even if it wasn't on purpose.*

He ignored the other voice. The one reminding him of the things he'd said, telling him Braeden wouldn't want him anymore. He couldn't let himself believe that or he'd go crazy.

When the urge to scream and cry subsided, he staggered to his feet and started walking.

Chapter Six

The portal twisted and disappeared, leaving Braeden with nothing but the tingle of energy against his fingertips. Joseph was gone. Suddenly, shockingly, impossibly gone.

How? He shouldn't be able to open a portal. He's learned nothing of that sort of magic yet.

Until this moment, Braeden hadn't even known whether or not Joseph would ever be able to access the Space unaided. That question, at least, was now answered.

Braeden shook himself. He could worry about how it had happened later. He hoped. Right now, he needed to deal with the fact that Joseph had somehow opened a doorway into the Space between the worlds and been drawn into it. Joseph knew nothing of how that strange place worked. Most likely he had no idea of how he'd gotten in, or of how to get out again. Braeden had to find him, and quickly. The Space was no place to linger.

Taking a deep breath, Braeden closed his eyes and focused his mind, searching for the link he'd created between himself and Joseph on that night so many years ago.

It wasn't there.

Fear spiked through Braeden's guts. His eyes flew open. If he couldn't track Joseph...

"Don't think of it," he admonished himself. "Try again."

Braeden sank down to sit cross-legged on the floor, then shut his eyes once more. He drew three slow, deep breaths, centering himself and clearing his mind, then attempted once again to find the thread of his connection to Joseph.

His lover's life force flared through his consciousness in a brief fiery burst, then faded and died away before he could grasp it.

Oh Danu, no. No.

His link with Joseph was gone. Braeden hoped it had been swallowed up by Joseph's innate magic. The alternative didn't bear thinking on.

He didn't waste any more time trying to resurrect the connection. Leaping to his feet, Braeden summoned his knife, spelled open a portal and flung himself into it.

Right away, he realized Joseph was not there. Very few of the Sidhe traveled between the human world and Tir-na-nog these days, and fewer still used the Space to travel place to place in a single world. Any being with faery blood would glow like a comet in this emptiness. If Joseph were here, Braeden would have known instantly.

Joseph must have found the way out, just as he had somehow found the way in.

Relieved, Braeden focused on timing his exit back into the human world. It had to be perfect, if he wanted to find Joseph quickly. Now that he knew Joseph wasn't trapped in the Space, he thought he knew where Joseph had gone. The fight they'd had just before the unexpected opening of the portal told him that much. But unless he left the Space at precisely the right moment, he could end up hundreds of miles from Joseph's childhood home, miles he'd have to cover in more conventional ways. He couldn't risk another trip through the Space, not without Joseph by his side. The chance of ending up even further away from him was too great.

Just as he was about to make the jump back to the human world, Braeden felt a malevolent presence in the Space. A deep red glow, more felt than seen, seeped through the nothingness around him. Hate, fear and lusts blacker than the Space swallowed Braeden in a seething mass, and his blood ran cold.

Caratacus. He was here, in the Space, surely as aware of Braeden's presence as Braeden was of his.

Ignoring the overwhelming need to go straight to Joseph in spite of the danger, Braeden bypassed his planned exit and instead opened a portal as far from his lover as he dared, intent on leading Caratacus away from Joseph. It was a tricky business. If we went too far, Caratacus would ignore him and instead follow the call of Joseph's magic to his. Caratacus's sense of his son's magic was too general to pinpoint his exact location, but once he'd narrowed Joseph's location to within a few miles he could home in on him. Braeden meant to keep Caratacus close enough to Joseph to believe he was on the right track, but far enough away that he wouldn't actually be able to find him.

Braeden tumbled out into the humid green twilight of a cypress swamp. The heat closed around him like a damp blanket, thick with the smell of stagnant water and decaying plants. Insects buzzed all around. A frog plopped into the dark pool at Braeden's feet, sending tiny ripples through the scum of algae floating on the water's surface.

Not far away, the crackle of a portal opening announced Caratacus's arrival. Braeden transfigured himself into a firefly and floated up into the branches over his head. The miniaturized knife clung to him by a spell, a comforting weight against his abdomen.

Below, Caratacus came into view, hovering over the ground with a lazy pulse of his wings. "You are naught but an insolent child, Joseph," he called, turning his head this way and that. "Do you truly believe your lover can keep you from me?"

Braeden settled on a branch and watched the murderer and usurper drift in a slow, searching circle. The four silent followers were nowhere in sight, but Braeden sensed their auras like an oily film over the bright energy of the living swamp. Having been tainted by dark and unnatural magic, the four nameless Sidhe and their lord had cast themselves out of the natural world. They could no longer make use of elemental earth magics, and their auras would no longer blend into the natural world. With practice and concentration, any of the Fae would be able to sense the faint differences between them and others of their kind. To Braeden, who possessed a talent for reading the energy of all living things, their presence was as obvious as a bloodstain on white linen.

Not for the first time, Braeden was glad Caratacus had never learned this about him.

They believe Joseph is still with me, Braeden mused as the four moved back and forth in a clear search pattern. *Caratacus senses him, but cannot find him, so they assume we are together. They mean to deceive us into thinking Caratacus is alone here, and take us by surprise while our attention is fixed on him. I mustn't let them know the truth.*

Beneath him, Caratacus settled his feet on the ground and turned his face up to the treetops. Braeden held perfectly still, just one more insect in a galaxy of them. Having cut themselves off from the Earth and her creatures, Caratacus and his followers wouldn't be able to sense him.

"Come, my son," Caratacus said, his voice a caricature of patience and reason. "I am your sire, and ruler of a mighty kingdom. A kingdom that you should inherit, by all rights. What falsehoods does the traitor Braeden Shay whisper to you when you lie together? Has he bespelled your mind as well as your body? I mean you no harm, Joseph. I want only to see you take your proper place at my side, as the future ruler of Tir-na-nog."

Braeden felt the spell of persuasion woven through Caratacus's words, and was thankful Joseph wasn't there. Strong he might be, and the spell wouldn't have the same power over him that it would over a true human, but Joseph hadn't yet developed the skill to guard his mind against such intrusions.

"Come with me now," Caratacus continued, green eyes scanning the maze of branches, "and I shall grant full pardon to Braeden, as proof of my mercy and goodwill."

One of Caratacus's men appeared from around the trunk of a huge old cypress. He shook his head in answer to the questioning look from his master. Caratacus hissed, long fingers clenching. "They are here," he growled. "Bring the others. We will cast a blood trace."

A blood trace?

Puzzled, Braeden studied the strange, multifaceted image of Caratacus he saw through his insect eyes. Blood tracing was ancient magic, not as dark as the spell binding Caratacus and his minions, but more obscure and infinitely more difficult to cast. All five would need to speak the spell in perfect unison, and all would be required to shed blood in precisely the same amounts. And most confounding of all, they would need some part of the one they wished to find. Blood worked best, but with their level of skill any part of the body would do. A scraping of skin, a lock of hair, any bodily fluid...

A jolt of fear shot up Braeden's spine as he remembered the cabin in Shining Rock Wilderness, the bed where he and Joseph had made love that morning, their mingled seed spilling on the rumpled sheets.

Caratacus and his disciples had been in the bedroom.

Oh, Danu.

If Caratacus were to cast a blood trace on Joseph, they would find him within moments. Braeden could not allow that.

Waiting was the hardest thing Braeden had ever done, but he forced himself to do it. He had to recover the semen he was certain they had gotten from the bed he and Joseph had shared, and in order to do that he had to know where it was.

After a moment, the other three Sidhe drifted silently to Caratacus's side. One took a torn bit of sheet from his pouch and laid it on the ground, while another drew an iron blade from a sheath at his side. It was time to act.

Before the five of them could begin the spell, Braeden gathered his magic and cast two spells of his own, in two different directions. Faint voices sounded from the east, the crash of human feet through undergrowth from the west.

Caratacus's head snapped up, whipping first one way then the other. He scanned the treetops once again, eyes narrowing, and Braeden held his breath. If this didn't work, he must be ready to go directly to Joseph and prepare them both for battle. He fluttered his wings and lifted one insect leg to touch the knife spelled to his abdomen.

A calculating smile spread across Caratacus's sharp features, and some of the tension ran out of Braeden's body. It seemed as though he was correct to gamble on Caratacus's arrogance.

"Do you hear?" Caratacus's question was directed at his followers, but his gaze darted this way and that through the thick press of trees. "It seems as though we will not have to perform the blood trace after all. Our quarry is near, and they are supremely careless. We will separate, each searching in a different direction. Hurry."

The four unnamed faeries each melted into the cypresses, heading for the four points of the compass. Caratacus remained, staring up into the treetop. One lifted brow and a slight smirk from him erased the last of Braeden's doubt. Caratacus had fallen neatly into Braeden's trap, believing Braeden was attempting to draw him and his men away in order to escape with Joseph.

Braeden would have laughed if his firefly form was capable of it. Caratacus clearly thought him incapable of any subtlety or strategic thinking. What Braeden actually had in mind would never occur to Caratacus.

Before Caratacus could summon the bit of sheet to him, Braeden made his move. A swift unspoken spell erased all traces of his and Joseph's mingled seed from the piece of fabric and replaced it with a smear of animal semen from the ground nearby.

Braeden watched as Caratacus closed his hand over the scrap of cotton, slipped into a tangle of vines and glamoured himself to blend into the greenery. If he hadn't been certain Caratacus would do exactly that, he would have believed the other had joined his companions in the search. He and Joseph, had the man actually been present, would have emerged from hiding only to find themselves on the receiving end of Caratacus's dark magic.

Suppressing a shudder, Braeden took to the air and fluttered off through the trees. There was no time to sit and contemplate what might have been, even had he been so inclined. If his guess was correct, he'd landed in the swamplands of coastal Louisiana, roughly thirty miles south of Joseph's home. His plan was to travel as a firefly until the cypress growth thinned, then change back to his true form and fly the remainder of the distance to Joseph. He needed the speed his faery wings would provide. With any luck, he and Joseph would be far away by the time Caratacus discovered he'd been deceived.

Within a few minutes, the thick growth began to open up. Braeden shed his insect form while still in the air and soared high above the trees. A moment to orient himself and a quick concealing glamour was all he needed. He shot off through the hot summer afternoon, on his way to the rambling old farmhouse where he'd first met the child who would one day shape his future.

It wasn't long before Braeden caught sight of the peaked green roof set amongst a grove of oaks below him. Spanish moss draped the branches, swaying in the hot breeze. He landed behind a particularly large tree, out of sight of the house, and cast a glamour to make himself look human. Tucking his knife into a sheath he'd conjured to his thigh, he started walking toward the house.

As he mounted the steps onto the wide porch, the front door opened and a woman emerged. Braeden's throat constricted. Evangeline. Joseph's mother. She looked almost exactly the same as she had when Braeden had first seen her, tall and shapely with an exotic beauty her only child had inherited. Only a few gray hairs, a few fine lines and eyes that had seen far too much distinguished her from the frightened young girl Caratacus had brought to Tir-na-nog over one hundred mortal years ago.

Hoping his glamour would conceal his true nature, Braeden stopped at the bottom of the steps and smiled. "Good afternoon, madam. I was wondering if—"

"What're you doing here?" Evangeline stalked forward, the gauzy yellow sundress she wore swirling around her legs. Her dark eyes, so like her son's, blazed with fear and fury. "Where's my boy?"

Braeden hung onto his casual expression with difficulty. "Pardon? I'm sure I don't—"

"You think I don't know a glamour when I see one? I know you're one of *them*." She spat the word as if it were poison. "And I know something's happened. Joey's boss called down here a week and a half ago wondering if I'd seen him. He got sick one day at work, and nobody's heard or seen anything of him since he left that day, two weeks ago. He's not called me, he's just disappeared, and that's not like him." Gathering her long skirt in one hand,

Evangeline descended the steps and pointed a slender finger in Braeden's face. "Now you tell me where he is, because I know you people are behind whatever's happened to him."

Braeden's heart sank. If Joseph wasn't here, he had no idea how to find him. "We became separated. I'd hoped he would be here."

She crossed her arms and glared. "Tell me what's happened to my son."

Sighing, Braeden sat on the bottom step and rested his head in his hands. "Joseph's powers came upon him the day he disappeared. I'd been watching him, so I was able to get him to safety before Caratacus could find him." Evangeline's soft, horrified gasp tore at Braeden's heart, but he didn't look up. "He's been with me, up until a short time ago. I've been trying to train him for what he must face, and he's learned much. But today, he accidentally opened a portal into the Space between the worlds, and I...I lost him. He wanted very badly to see you. I'd hoped that desire would take him here."

Silence fell. Braeden closed his eyes and listened to the sounds of birds and insects and leaves in the breeze. There was a rustle of fabric, then slim fingers grabbed his chin, forcing his face up. He opened his eyes to meet Evangeline's needle-sharp gaze.

"Didn't you tell him he couldn't come here?" she asked, her voice surprisingly calm. "Caratacus isn't above using me to get to Joseph."

"Indeed, I did tell him." A faint smile tugged at the corner of Braeden's mouth, even as his heart twisted. "He was most displeased."

She laughed, the sound sharp and humorless. "He never was good at taking no for an answer when he really wanted something." Shaking her head, she let go of Braeden's chin and pressed her fingers to her cheek. Only the faint tremor in her hand gave away the fear Braeden knew she must be feeling. "I hoped this would never happen. But I had a feeling it would, one day."

The sadness and resignation in her voice made Braeden's chest tight. Acting on impulse, he took her hand and squeezed it. "I'm sorry. I would change it if I could. For both of you."

She didn't answer. For a moment they sat in silence, staring at each other, her slim hand caught in Braeden's. He had no idea what to say. Joseph's life had been in his hands, and he'd let the man slip away from him. If it meant Joseph came to harm, he'd never forgive himself, and he knew Evangeline wouldn't either.

She drew a shuddering breath and opened her mouth as if to speak. Then she stiffened, her eyes going wide. Before Braeden could say a word, she ripped her hand from his, gathered her skirts around her thighs and went running through the trees.

Braeden stood, intending to go after her. He turned just in time to see her fling herself into the arms of a naked man with long black hair and creamy mocha skin which Braeden knew to be smooth, warm and soft.

Joseph had come home after all.

Weak with relief, Braeden leaned against the porch step railing and watched Joseph and Evangeline walk toward him with their arms around each other, Evangeline laughing through the tears streaming down her cheeks. Joseph was smiling, but he looked tired and a bit glassy-eyed.

Braeden bit his lip as Joseph kissed his mother's cheek, let go of her and approached him. It was all he could do to keep from reaching out and gathering his lover into his arms. He had no idea if Evangeline knew of her son's sexuality or not, and he didn't want to give Joseph further cause to hate him.

Joseph stared at Braeden, a maelstrom of emotions swirling in his eyes. "I was hoping you'd come here."

"And I hoped you would as well." Braeden wished his voice wouldn't shake so. "Thank Danu you're all right."

Joseph didn't answer. Instead, he wound both arms around Braeden's neck and kissed him.

Braeden couldn't hold back the sob of relief welling in his throat. After what had happened just before Joseph disappeared, he'd expected more harsh words, more accusations. His relief at having Joseph in his arms again was huge. He clutched Joseph close and opened his mouth for his lover's insistent tongue.

When they pulled apart at last, Joseph cradled Braeden's face in his hands and gazed into his eyes with a directness that was almost painful in its intensity. "I love you, Braeden," Joseph whispered, his fingers winding through Braeden's hair. "I'm sorry about before. I didn't mean it. Please forgive me."

Braeden smiled, his heart singing. "There is nothing to forgive, *a chuisle*. My heart is fully in your keeping. I have been yours for years, though you did not know it."

Tilting his head sideways, Joseph gave Braeden a curious look. "That's what you said earlier, isn't it? That phrase in Gaelic, when we were making love on the floor. You were telling me you love me."

"Indeed, yes." Braeden laid a hand on Joseph's cheek, thumb caressing the corner of his mouth. "I do love you, *a chuisle*. My pulse. My heart. I love you more than anything in this life, and I always will."

The pure happiness in Joseph's eyes at that moment sent Braeden's spirit soaring. Joseph pressed a single fingertip to Braeden's bottom lip, leaned forward and kissed the spot he'd just touched. The tip of his tongue flicked out, and Braeden let out a soft moan.

The sound of the front door slamming made them jump. Braeden looked up to the porch and met Evangeline's cool, appraising gaze with a wince. He'd been so caught up in Joseph, he'd forgotten all about her. She set down the two suitcases she carried and planted her hands on her hips.

"Evangeline." Braeden's cheeks flushed, wondering how much she knew, or had guessed, before this moment. "I should explain this."

"Nothing to explain." Digging in her skirt pocket, she produced a key and locked the front door. "If you and

Joey are...well, intimate, you know he's not one to keep things to himself. He told me he was gay when he was thirteen." She quirked an eyebrow at Braeden as she put the key back in her pocket. "He could do worse than you. Has done, in fact. Some of the boys he brought home in high school were enough to curdle a mother's blood. You? I like."

Braeden smiled. "Thank you."

"Mama, what's with the suitcases?" Joseph asked, disengaging himself from Braeden's embrace and hurrying up the steps to help his mother carry her bags. "Are you going someplace?"

"It's not safe for me to stay here anymore. Not safe for me, and definitely not safe for you. I think you know why." She shook her head. "I've been getting ready for this day ever since your boss first called me and told me you'd disappeared. I was scared to death, but I hoped you'd turn up here eventually. Never thought you'd turn up naked as the day you were born, though."

Joseph hunched his shoulders. "Sorry. It all happened sort of fast. I didn't have time to get Braeden to make any clothes for me."

"Hold still, Joseph, and I'll clothe you now." With a wave of his hand, Braeden conjured jeans, a T-shirt and a pair of running shoes. "There you are, love."

"Thanks." Joseph gave Braeden a heart-melting smile before turning back to his mother. "So you're leaving?"

"Yes, I am. I'm all set up to stay with Mimi Vallens in San Antonio. You remember her, don't you, baby? She used to be in my bridge club before she and John moved last year."

"Yeah, I remember." Leaning against the railing behind him, Joseph stared at his mother with frank curiosity. "Will you come back?"

"I hope so, when this whole thing is over." Stepping closer, she patted Joseph's cheek. "Help me with my bags, will you? I can take you and..." She frowned and turned to look at Braeden. "I'm sorry, what's your name?"

"Braeden Shay." Braeden walked up the steps and picked up one of her suitcases. "We met once, years ago. The night you left Tir-na-nog. I'm not surprised you do not remember."

"Hm. I'd probably recognize you without the glamour." She drew a deep breath and blew it out. "I can take you boys wherever you need to go. But I think we should leave right away."

"You're right." Hefting his mother's second bag, Joseph started down the steps. "Let's go, before I start getting all sentimental."

Braeden followed Joseph and his mother to Evangeline's sedan and tossed the suitcase into the trunk along with the other bag. Evangeline slid behind the wheel and started the engine. Joseph climbed into the front seat beside her, while Braeden got in the back.

Joseph twisted in his seat to watch the house recede into the distance as the car rolled down the long gravel drive. His dark eyes brimmed with memories, and his expression was wistful.

Taking his hand, Braeden kissed it, then laid the palm against his cheek. "You'll come back here, *a chuisle.* If it is within my power, you will return to this place one day, I swear it."

Joseph said nothing, but the faint smile curving his mouth was enough. Leaning over, Joseph pressed a soft kiss to Braeden's lips, then settled sideways in the seat, his fingers wound through Braeden's.

༓

After a short discussion, Evangeline drove Joseph and Braeden all the way to the New Orleans airport. Braeden still wanted to go to the jungle as he'd planned, but he didn't feel it was safe to travel through the Space between worlds just yet. Using conventional rather than magical means of transport seemed like a good solution. Caratacus wouldn't be expecting it. If they flew to Venezuela then trekked overland through the jungle, they would essentially disappear for several days. Since he'd been the one who created the magical shelter in the impenetrable jungle south of the Orinoco River, Braeden could feel it in his mind. He would be able to take them directly there.

He'd always been confident of his ability to keep Joseph safe in the jungle, even all those years ago, before he knew what Joseph's powers would be. Now, he knew they would be safer there than anywhere else. Joseph's magical connection to the plant kingdom provided them with a constant source of protection.

When they reached the airport, Evangeline parked the car at the curb in front of the ticket lobby. Her eyes shone with tears as she turned to her son and hugged him hard. "Be careful, baby," she said, her voice shaking. "I love you."

"I love you too, Mama." Joseph kissed her forehead and pulled away, wiping his eyes. "I'll get in touch with you as soon as it's safe."

"You do that. But not until it *is* safe, all right? Not until he's…"

She trailed off, but all three of them knew what she meant. Joseph smiled sadly and touched her cheek. "I promise."

She squeezed Joseph's hand, then glanced over at Braeden. "You take care of my boy."

"I swear I will do everything in my power to protect him," Braeden said, holding her gaze so she would see the truth of it in his eyes.

Nodding, she drew a deep breath and gave a trembling smile. "You boys better go on now. The less anyone sees of us together, the better."

"Yeah, I guess." Joseph reached out and pulled his mother into another hug. He held on for a long moment, sniffling against her shoulder, then let go and jumped out of the car before she could say anything.

Braeden started to slide across the seat and open the car door. Evangeline reached toward him, and he stopped. "Evangeline?"

"Do you love him?" she asked, her expression pleading.

"With all my heart," he answered honestly. "I would lay down my life for him."

She nodded. "Goodbye, Braeden. I hope we meet again, in this life."

"As do I." Taking her hand, he kissed her fingers. "Goodbye."

He felt her gaze on him as he exited the car and slid his arm around Joseph's shoulders. She waved and blew them a kiss, then put the car in gear and pulled away.

Joseph watched the car until it was out of sight. He didn't say anything, but the way he clung to Braeden—not to mention the way his chest hitched—spoke volumes.

"Are you all right, my love?" Braeden asked, nuzzling Joseph's hair.

"I will be. It's just hard, knowing what might happen. Knowing we might not ever see each other again." Sighing, Joseph tilted his head to look Braeden in the eye. "So, we're going to South America, right?"

"Yes. I'd like to fly into San Fernando if we can. That is the closest city to our destination."

Joseph nodded. "How do we get to this place of yours? Hike?"

"Exactly." Braeden smiled, remembering the spot he'd chosen, so deep in the jungle even the native tribes didn't go there. "It's beautiful there, Joseph. There are trees and flowering vines such as you've never seen, things that grow nowhere else in this world."

A spark of excitement flared to life in Joseph's eyes, glowing behind the fear and sadness. "Let's go get our plane tickets. Oh by the way, what do we use for money?"

"I shall conjure some."

Joseph touched Braeden's cheek. "Come on. I really just want to get out of here right now."

"Of course." Pressing a kiss to Joseph's temple, Braeden took his hand and led him toward the terminal doorway and the next stage of their journey.

Chapter Seven

"Fuck." Joey stared down into the leafy green gulf at his feet. "How the hell do we get across?"

Beside him, Braeden shook his head. "There used to be a footbridge here."

"Yeah, well, it looks like it's gone." Gesturing the tangle of undergrowth aside, Joey edged sideways along the narrow strip of open space between the jungle and the ravine blocking their path. "Here's the posts and some rope." He bent and lifted the frayed end of what looked like homemade rope. "Looks like this is all that's left."

"Perhaps it rotted." Braeden frowned, wings fluttering like they always did when he was frustrated or just thinking hard. "I can't imagine it would have been deliberately destroyed."

"Not that it matters. However it happened, it's not here anymore, which leaves us with my original question." Dropping the rope, Joey went to Braeden and took his hand. "How do we get across?"

Braeden sighed. "I do not know."

Shit. I didn't expect that. Not knowing what to say, Joey gazed down into the narrow ravine. It looked like a fold in the vivid green fabric of the Venezuelan jungle. The sound of running water drifted from below, echoing up through the narrow canyon, muffled and distorted by a riot of greenery. An unnamed tributary of the Orinoco, Braeden had told him. The water itself was hidden by leaves and vines, and the mist from what sounded like vicious rapids.

A tug on his hair made Joey jump. He laughed when he felt the gentle, curious touch of a plant's consciousness in his mind. He thought out to the vine, and it unwound itself from his hair.

"Amazing."

Braeden's tone was soft and reverent. Surprised, Joey blinked at him. "What?"

"The way you are able to communicate with the growing things of this world." Braeden smiled, the mix of heat and love in his silvery eyes making Joey's skin burn. "You amaze me at every turn."

Joey's insides tightened, the way they did every time Braeden looked at him like that. Like he was the most beautiful, astounding creature in the universe. He didn't understand how someone like Braeden—a Sidhe warrior, powerful and dangerous and so lovely it hurt—could possibly look at him that way.

Unable to voice his feelings, Joey took Braeden's hand, hoping he would somehow understand what was in Joey's heart. The three days they'd spent trekking through the pathless jungle had only strengthened the bond between them. Joey felt that if they tried hard enough, they'd be able to read each other's minds.

The tender shine in Braeden's eyes said he understood Joey perfectly. He smiled, pulled Joey close and kissed his hair. "We must think of a way to reach the other side. If we can cross, we can reach the shelter tonight."

"Mm." Closing his eyes, Joey rested his head in the curve of Braeden's shoulder, enjoying the soft touch of his lover's hand on his back, sliding around his side to stroke his belly...

...until he realized one of Braeden's hands was still clutched in his own, and Braeden's other arm rested across his shoulders, fingers playing with his hair. His eyes flew open as the cool, tickly touch which wasn't Braeden's crept beneath the waist of his jeans.

"Holy shit." Drawing away from Braeden's embrace, Joey gently extracted the vine from his pants. "This plant's groping me."

Braeden laughed. "As I've said, all growing things are drawn to you. To your power."

"Yeah." A thought struck Joey. Holding the slender green whip in front of his face, he gave it a considering look. "I wonder if I can use that somehow to cross this ravine."

"I wondered that as well." Braeden ran a fingertip along the smooth skin of the vine. "This little one has the will, I can tell. But it hasn't the strength."

"There's lots of Ayahuasca in the jungle." Joey gestured toward the green shadows behind him. "They're strong."

"Indeed." Letting go of Joey's hand, Braeden spread his wings and lifted himself into the air. He rose upward to hover before a clump of leaves reaching for the sunlight. "Yes, there are many of them close by. It is a willful thing, the spirit vine. But fierce and faithful once tamed." He turned in midair, his hair flying around him. "Can you tame it, *a chuisle?*"

"I think so, yeah." Joey tipped his head back to smile at Braeden. "Come down here and talk to me."

Braeden flashed the mischievous grin which always made Joey feel warm inside. "Why? Does it distract you when I fly?"

"You know it does." Laughing, Joey stood on tiptoe and reached up to tickle Braeden's bare foot. "Come down. Please."

Braeden obediently drifted back to earth and pulled Joey into his arms. "I think you have an unnatural attraction to my wings."

"It's perfectly natural," Joey protested. He caressed one of Braeden's wings, and it vibrated under his fingertips. "God, I love that."

"What?" Braeden's voice had become husky, his eyes heavy-lidded.

"How turned on you get when I touch your wings." He did it again, tearing a moan from Braeden. "Who knew wings were an erogenous zone?"

"Mine have never been before." Braeden bent his head and pressed his cheek to Joey's. "Only you do this to me, my love. Only you."

"Oh." Swallowing the lump that rose in his throat, Joey wound a hand into Braeden's thick hair. "I never know what to say when you tell me those things. I can't describe how it makes me feel."

"You needn't say anything," Braeden told him. "I know."

Nodding, Joey brushed a quick kiss across Braeden's mouth before pulling away. Time was pressing, and they still had a long way to go.

"So what should we do?" Joey asked, eyeing the ravine. "I can get the spirit vines to do what I want, but the thing is I don't know what to ask them to do. They can hold my weight, I think, but I don't think any of them are long enough to reach all the way across."

"Hm." Braeden walked to the edge of the precipice and stood there gazing across the misty green space with a frown. "I don't believe the gap itself is more than thirty feet across. But in order for one of our growing friends to act as a bridge, it would have to cross another five or six feet to the closest sturdy tree and still have enough length to wrap securely around it. You are correct, I don't believe there are any spirit vines that long close enough to the edge to do us any good."

"Well, fuck." Joey ran a frustrated hand through his hair. It was greasy and tangled, with bits of earth and leaves stuck in it, and he wished he could wash it. "I don't guess you could fly us both across."

"Unfortunately, no. Were you a small child, I could carry you, but my wings cannot hold the extra weight of a grown man."

"Damn. Well, maybe we can—"

"Wait a moment." Braeden whirled around, looking determined. "Stay right here. I am going to fly into the ravine."

Joey raised his eyebrows. "How come?"

"I want to see what's down there. Perhaps it is possible to climb down and ascend the other side."

Joey doubted that, but he nodded. "Okay. But hurry, and be careful."

"I will." Grabbing Joey by the shoulders, Braeden kissed him hard. "I shall return in a moment and tell you what I find."

Joey watched as Braeden rose into the air with a beat of his wings, turned and dove into the chasm. *Please be okay,* he thought, staring at the spot where the mist swirled in the wake of Braeden's passing. He had no idea why he felt so nervous about Braeden flying down there— Braeden could certainly look after himself—but he couldn't help it. Watching his lover disappear where he couldn't follow made his stomach churn with fear.

It seemed like he stood there for ages, chewing his thumbnail and shifting from foot to foot. When Braeden reappeared, his hair dripping with condensation, Joey was so relieved he almost missed the wide smile on

Braeden's face. He flung himself at Braeden the moment his feet touched the ground, clutching him close.

Braeden chuckled and wrapped his arms around Joey. "Were you worried, love?"

"Yes." Loosening his grip, Joey pulled back enough to look into Braeden's eyes. "Maybe it's weird, but I don't like letting you out of my sight, even for a second."

"I understand. I feel the same." Braeden brushed a hunk of dirty, tangled hair away from Joey's face. "I believe I found a way for you to cross."

"Yeah? What is it?"

"About twenty-five feet down and upstream a bit, the ravine narrows quite a lot. It looks as though there was once a natural bridge of earth there, and it has eroded over the years. You should actually be able to step across."

Joey nodded. "Okay. And I guess I could climb down to that spot using a spirit vine. But how do I get up the other side?"

"There's a groove in the ground on the opposite side, sloping down to a spot just above the narrow place in the ravine." Braeden gestured upstream, toward a spot that looked exactly like every other spot of jungle. "It looks like a natural water chute. If it were raining right now, it would likely be unusable. But the weather's clear, and likely to remain so for a while. I believe you will be able to climb up, with the aid of vines on the other side."

"Sounds like a plan." Casting a wary look at the misty gulf, Joey twirled a strand of Braeden's hair nervously around his finger. "So. How deep is this thing, anyway?"

Braeden's expression grew serious. "At least two hundred feet."

Joey winced. "Fuck."

Cupping Joey's chin in one hand, Braeden stared hard into his eyes. "Listen to me. I will not let you fall. You can do this, Joseph."

Yes. I can do this. Joey swallowed. "I know."

"The morning is waning. We should get started."

"Yeah." Joey took a deep breath and let it out slowly, forcing himself to stay calm. "Show me the right spot."

Taking his hand, Braeden led him about twenty-five feet upstream. "Here. The jungle grows very close to the edge here. It should be simple enough to find a good sturdy vine that will allow itself to be bent to your will."

Joey looked around. The jungle loomed only steps away, its shade falling across the narrow strip of grass between the trees and the edge of the chasm. Just inside, Joey could see a twisted tangle of thick, sturdy spirit vines winding deep into the shadows. Perfect.

Shaking off the nervous tension as best he could, Joey let his mind relax and his consciousness expand the way Braeden had taught him. Instantly, he felt the spirit vines' awareness of him. He also felt their wildness, the untamable essence which made this vine sacred to so many, and doubt seized him. Could he really do this?

Could he control a being which had made this jungle its own for millennia?

A picture of his mother's face rose in his mind's eye, closely followed by the terrifying vision of Caratacus reaching out for him, fingers like claws and eyes full of murderous intent. He squared his shoulders. He could do this. He had no choice.

Concentrating on the oldest, strongest vine, Joey sent out a pulse of command as strong as he could summon, showing the creature exactly what he required. The response was startling. With a hiss like a hundred snakes, the vine whipped loose of the trees and undergrowth and slithered over the edge of the ravine.

Joey stared. "Wow."

"Surely this does not surprise you, *a chuisle.*" Smiling, Braeden squeezed Joey's hand. "You are very powerful, and you have already learned impressive control of that power. This is no more than I expected."

Joey kissed Braeden's fingers. "Thanks for that."

"It's simply the truth."

"Let's hope so." Dropping Braeden's hand, Joey sat beside the spot where the vine disappeared over the edge of the fissure and swung his legs into empty space. "Okay. Here I go."

As Joey grasped the vine and turned to face the earth bank, Braeden rose into the air and hovered beside him. Joey's heart hammered against his ribs, and he could hear the blood rushing in his ears. Focusing on the steady beat of Braeden's wings stirring the moist air, Joey began lowering himself into the gorge.

It didn't take but a few minutes to reach the spot he was aiming for. Joey breathed a silent thanks for the hours of physical training Braeden had put him through in the past weeks. If it wasn't for that, he figured his arms and legs would've been shaking uncontrollably by now. He settled himself carefully on the outcropping of roots and soil and let out a long breath.

Grabbing hold of a protruding root and fluttering his wings for balance, Braeden settled one foot on the ground beside Joey. "Give me your hand, Joseph. I'll steady you so you can turn around."

Joey took the hand Braeden offered and shuffled his feet in a careful circle. The shelf of land he stood on was roughly four square feet, large enough to stand on comfortably. The ground, however, was rough and uneven, and sloped alarmingly toward the chasm at his feet.

Facing the other side of the ravine, Joey did his best to ignore the drop below him and assess the situation. The wall of earth across the way bulged outward, coming within a couple of feet of touching the outcropping where he stood. The crevice Braeden had told him about opened roughly four feet above the ledge on the other side, carving a straight channel up through the earth. The firm-packed soil of the channel looked smooth enough to worry Joey, but the slope was quite shallow. He should be able to climb it.

"I can do this," he muttered, wondering whether he was talking to Braeden or himself. He shot a quick glance at Braeden. "The ground doesn't feel too stable here. Can you help me cross?"

"Bring down a vine on the other side," Braeden instructed. "I'll hold on to it and steady you as you step over."

"Yeah, good idea. Okay."

Forcing the tension from his mind, Joey thought out to the many spirit vines whose presence he felt in the jungle across the way. Instantly, a vine as thick as his forearm came tumbling down from above.

"It's not long enough to reach over here," Joey observed, frowning. "I wanted to use it for a safety rope."

"Then I shall be your safety rope." Letting go of his hand, Braeden flew across to settle on the opposite ledge. He looped the vine twice around his wrist, got a good grip on it, and leaned across the gulf with his free hand held out. "Take my hand, love."

Joey gulped. Safety was only a few feet away. All he had to do was take two steps forward. Braeden was right there to help him. But the water roared under his feet and those two steps felt like miles. His knees shook, and he hated it. Hated his own weakness.

"There is no shame in fear," Braeden said, his voice soft and calm. "But I'll not let you fall, love. Remember that."

Joey gave him a weak smile. "You can read my mind, can't you?"

"I have no need to read your mind, when your face is a mirror for your heart." Braeden waggled his fingers, his gaze locked with Joey's. "Come, *a chuisle*. Take my hand."

Biting his lip, Joey took a cautious step forward, then another, never once looking away from Braeden's face. Braeden's fingers closed around his wrist in a strong and reassuring grip, and Joey felt some of his fear dissolve. He grasped Braeden's wrist, held his breath and lifted his right foot to step across the void.

He hadn't yet gotten a foothold on the opposite ledge when the ground beneath his left foot crumbled. Before he quite knew what had happened, he found himself dangling over the mist-shrouded depths. Only Braeden's iron grip on his wrist kept him from falling. Swinging his other hand up, he clamped it onto Braeden's arm and tried to pull himself onto the ledge, but he wasn't strong enough.

"Help me," he pleaded, sounding as panicked as he felt. "I can't get up, Braeden."

"Joseph, the vines," Braeden gasped, the strain of holding Joey's weight crystal clear in his voice. "Call more vines, quickly."

Joey's frantic thought brought dozens of spirit vines and a few other species cascading down the slope from both sides of the ravine. He focused his will just in time to avoid being torn apart by many different plants trying to pull him in several directions at once. Two old, sturdy spirit vines from the side he was trying to reach wrapped around him and hauled him through the air, wrenching his hand from Braeden's. The world swung around him in a dizzy arc. The vines deposited him on his feet just under the trees at the edge of the fissure, and everything righted itself again.

Joey stood there panting, heart racing with the shock of what had almost happened. Braeden zoomed out of the chasm, hit the ground running and swept Joey into his arms. Joey clung to him, shaking all over.

"Are you all right, my love?" Braeden's hands smoothed up and down Joey's back. He pressed a kiss to Joey's temple. "Are you injured?"

Joey shook his head. "No, I'm fine. Just scared shitless, is all." He laid his head on Braeden's shoulder and closed his eyes, relaxing in his lover's embrace. "I shouldn't have tried to cross until I found vines long enough to use as safety ropes. I hope I didn't hurt you, making you take all my weight with one hand like that."

"I am unharmed, never fear." Braeden fell silent. Joey could feel the thud of Braeden's heart, almost as fast as his own. When Braeden spoke again, his voice was ragged. "I do not know what I would do if I lost you."

Joey wanted to promise that they would never lose each other. That they'd always be together, they'd defeat Caratacus and live happily ever after. But they weren't guaranteed victory. Caratacus might very well kill them both. Braeden knew that as well as he did. Probably better.

Unable to provide reassurance to Braeden or himself, Joey held Braeden tight, stroking his wings. It would have to be enough, for now.

CB

They reached the shelter Braeden had prepared just as the sun dipped below the tree line. Joey stood with Braeden beside a large boulder on the bank of one of the many tributaries of the Orinoco, staring in frank dismay at the waterfall thundering down from somewhere so high over his head he couldn't even see it in the gathering dusk.

"So what you're telling me," he said, clutching Braeden's hand in a death grip, "is that we have to go through that waterfall?"

Braeden nodded. "Yes."

"That one right there? The one so big and loud it's hurting my ears? The one about fifty feet wide that looks like it could pound this boulder into sand? That waterfall?"

"Yes." Laughing, Braeden lifted Joey's hand and kissed his knuckles. "Do not worry, love. My magic will take us through unharmed."

Joey leaned against Braeden's shoulder. Logically, he knew Braeden was telling the truth. His instinct for self-preservation was a bit harder to convince.

"What's behind it?" he asked, hoping Braeden wouldn't realize he was stalling for time to work up his courage.

"There is a cavern winding far into the earth. I have placed spells to hide it from the casual observer." Braeden smiled, silver-gray eyes twinkling. "You are stalling, *a chuisle*. Do you not trust me?"

"Of course I trust you." Snagging a handful of Braeden's hair, Joey pulled his face down for a long, deep kiss. "Okay, what do we do?"

"Just keep hold of my hand, and stay close. And remember, this is magic. Things are not always as they seem."

Joey didn't feel entirely comforted by this, but he nodded and forced a smile. He *did* trust Braeden, with all his heart. It was life he didn't always trust.

He was surprised when Braeden led him into the clear, cool water eddying against the riverbank. He'd expected Braeden to take some hidden pathway behind the falls. "Braeden?"

"I have created a few selected illusions about this place." Braeden turned to smile over his shoulder at Joey. "Stretch out your senses, Joseph. Your eyes are easily deceived, but your instincts are not. Trust what your heart tells you."

Joey frowned, but followed Braeden into the river. The water swirled around his knees, and he was beginning to wonder if they'd be forced to swim, when his foot lifted of its own accord and planted itself on something solid.

Something he couldn't see. He gaped, unbelieving, as Braeden led him out of the water, up a shallow slope of seemingly thin air.

"I don't fucking believe this," he mumbled, staring at the river churning beneath his feet. "What is this, Braeden? Are we really walking on air, or is there land here and you glamoured it invisible?"

"A bit of both, actually. There is a string of large rocks that rise far enough above the water to walk on. I added a bit of magical reinforcement into the glamour, to make the way smooth and safe since it's unseen." Braeden stopped a few steps from the thundering water of the fall. He raised a hand and muttered a few words in Gaelic, and the water parted to reveal a wall of dark, wet stone. "Do not be fooled, love. The wall is an illusion."

"Yeah, I kind of figured." Joey followed Braeden through the watery arch, staring wide-eyed at the river cascading around him. The level rays of the setting sun pierced through the trees to catch in the spray from the waterfall, turning it into a shimmering rainbow. "Wow. It's beautiful here."

"Indeed, it is." In the shallow stone concavity behind the fall, Braeden turned and spoke a counterspell, and the water closed in a nearly solid curtain that cut off the failing light. "You are going to love the place where we're headed, *a chuisle.*"

Joey smiled at the vague blur of Braeden's face in the dimness. "I sure am ready to be there. Is it far?"

"No." With a swift flick of Braeden's fingers, the stone wall wavered and vanished, revealing a narrow passage that twisted into the dark. "A short walk will bring us there."

Before Joey could ask how they were supposed to find their way in the dark, Braeden waved a hand and a row of torches along one wall flickered to life. The stone gleamed wetly in the golden light.

Hand in hand, they walked down the rough-hewn passage. The roar of the waterfall faded steadily behind them. By the time Braeden led him into a second passage that yawned suddenly to his right, Joey could no longer hear it at all. The sharp wet scent of the river, however, was as strong as ever. Puzzled, Joey drew a deep breath. The distinct aroma of night-blooming flowers came to him, mixed with the musky tang of damp earth and the fresh smell of greenery.

"Where are we going?" he asked, realizing with wonder that he could once again hear the merry tinkle of falling water.

Braeden turned and smiled at him as they rounded a sharp bend. "Here. Look."

Joey looked, and stopped dead in his tracks, his mouth falling open. "Oh my God. Braeden. Wow."

Slipping an arm around Joey's shoulders, Braeden pulled him close and kissed his brow. "Lovely, is it not? The closest thing to my home to be found in this world."

Joey could only nod and stare at the little bubble of paradise Braeden had found. Or created? Joey wasn't sure, and it didn't matter. The place was like something out of a storybook. High earthen banks covered in spirit vines and flowers hemmed in a rough oval about the size of a baseball diamond. On the opposite end from where they stood, a short waterfall tumbled about ten feet into a small pool. A stream leapt from the pool, wound through the grass carpeting the hollow, chattered over a jumble of small stones to Joey's right and plunged into a gap in the rock from which he and Braeden had just emerged.

Beside the pool, huddled beneath a tremendous banyan whose roots hung like a living ladder down the sheer wall, sat a cozy three-sided shelter of bamboo roofed with balsa leaves. Shadows and distance veiled the interior, but Joey knew Braeden well enough by now to know the place would be simple, but comfortable.

"Joseph?" Braeden tilted Joey's face toward him with two fingers beneath his chin. "What do you think, love?"

Joey grinned. "Can we live here forever?"

"Perhaps we should not think that far ahead at this point." Braeden leaned down and kissed Joey's lips. "There is soapberry growing in abundance here. Shall we have a wash in the pool before retiring?"

"Oh fuck yeah," Joey groaned. "I'm filthy. Most soapberry seed pods are pretty poisonous, can we grind these up for soap without making ourselves sick?"

"Certainly. We would have to ingest them in order to be poisoned, and even then I doubt it would cause more than transient digestive upset." Braeden started through the luxurious grass toward the shelter, and Joey trailed behind him, still holding his hand. "The soapberry that grows in this place seems to be a subspecies of one of the types which flourish in these jungles. I've found that the seed pods of this particular variety are not only less poisonous than other types, but the soap they produce is also milder."

"Sounds perfect." A shiver ran through Joey's body at the thought of being clean for the first time in days. "Where are the soapberry trees? I want to get started on that right away."

"There is a cluster of them on the other side of the pool." Braeden nodded toward a clump of low, spreading trees opposite the shelter. Raising a hand, he muttered something under his breath and twisted his wrist. "There. I've picked a sufficient number of seed pods in the correct stage of development. They are waiting beside the pool. We have but to grind them with the stones from the river, and we can bathe."

"Fantastic." Jumping in front of Braeden, Joey wound both arms around his neck and kissed him, walking backward so they wouldn't have to stop. "Can I wash your wings?"

Laughing, Braeden grabbed Joey's ass in both hands and squeezed. "Once again, I am forced to conclude that your fascination with my wings is abnormally strong."

"Okay, well, I *did* get a giant tattoo of them," Joey conceded, nipping Braeden's chin. "So. Now that I've admitted I'm fixated on your wings, can I wash them?"

"But the way you touch them fills me with such desire, I cannot think." Braeden's fingers dug into Joey's buttocks, kneading them in a way that made Joey's heartbeat stutter. "I will surely beg you to make love to me right there in the pool."

"And this is a problem how?" Dipping his head, Joey bit the curve of Braeden's neck, in the spot that always made him quiver with pleasure. "I can't think of a more romantic place for it."

"True." Braeden stopped walking, and Joey realized they'd reached the edge of the pool. Pulling Joey tight against him, Braeden captured his mouth in a hungry kiss. "Let us hurry, my beauty," he whispered. "Already the need for you consumes me."

Joey moaned, his head falling back to bare his neck for Braeden's kisses. "God, Braeden. I love how you talk to me."

"I love the way you touch me," Braeden answered, his voice soft and heavy. His fingers trailed up Joey's spine, then back down again to dip between his buttocks. "I love the way you taste, the way you smell, the music of your sighs when you're inside me." One hand clenched in Joey's hair, holding his head still while Braeden licked a long, wet line up his throat. "*Tá tú go h-álainn, a chuisle.*"

Vague shades of meaning flitted through Joey's mind, setting a hot glow in his belly. Straddling Braeden's thigh, Joey ground their hips together. "What're you saying, Braeden?"

"You're beautiful," Braeden murmured, lips trailing fire across Joey's skin. "I love you."

A soft, sobbing cry broke from Joey's mouth when Braeden's long, slender finger breached him, the lack of lubrication causing a pleasurable burn. "Oh. God, I can't... I need..."

Braeden nodded, his finger twisting inside Joey and sending fiery waves of sensation through him. "We will bathe later. Make love to me, Joseph."

Tremors shivered up Joey's spine. Cupping Braeden's cheek in one palm, he devoured his lover's mouth, tongue plunging deep to taste Braeden's need. Without breaking the kiss, he began walking them into the gloom under the trees.

He felt the presence of the vines, an unfamiliar species of liana, long before their rough skins touched his. The sudden, vivid mental picture which burst in his mind morphed into a command before he consciously realized it. Fear flared bright behind his eyelids for a moment before his confidence reasserted itself. His control over the local plant life was absolute, fine-tuned and perfect. The incident with crossing the gorge had proven that. He had nothing to fear, and neither did Braeden.

Braeden let out a surprised cry when supple green tendrils sprouted from the thick, woody vines and wound around his wrists, gently tugging his arms behind his back. "Joseph?"

"It's okay," Joey promised, stroking Braeden's face. "They won't hurt you. I won't let them."

Braeden stared at him, eyes bright in the waning twilight. "My body is yours, my love. Do with it what you will. I trust you."

The thrill of having Braeden completely at his mercy made Joey's head spin. Framing Braeden's face in his hands, he pressed a kiss to his lips. "Thank you, Braeden. I love you."

Braeden seemed about to speak, but the words were lost in a sharp gasp as liana vines slithered around him from all directions. Joey stepped back, his thought directing the liana as they wove themselves together beneath Braeden's body, lifting him right off the ground. Within seconds, Braeden hung suspended in a living cradle. Newly sprouted green shoots corkscrewed around his thighs and knees, pulling his legs up and apart. His arms remained behind his back, wrists bound by slender, supple tendrils.

The sight of Braeden like that, restrained, spread and exposed, stole Joey's breath. He stared at his lover's engorged and leaking cock, his quivering wings and parted lips, and wished he had the power to stop time. To hold Braeden in this state of anticipation, prolonging his excitement forever.

"Joseph," Braeden moaned, his head falling back so that his hair nearly brushed the forest floor. "Please. Please."

"Undress me," Joey ordered. "And conjure the lube."

Lifting his head, Braeden closed his eyes, brows drawing together in concentration. His lips formed the familiar words of the necessary spells. Joey's filthy T-shirt and jeans and ragged sneakers vanished, leaving his skin bare to the warm, damp air. The little bottle of oil appeared in the grass at his feet. He scooped it up, then stepped between Braeden's splayed legs.

Joey laid a hand on Braeden's thigh and flipped up the cap of the oil vial with the other hand. "Open your eyes, Braeden. Look at me."

Braeden obeyed, his gaze instantly locking with Joey's. The heat in his eyes nearly made Joey's knees buckle. He drew a few shallow breaths, trying to keep control of himself. "God, Braeden. Just looking at you like this makes me want to come."

"No," Braeden growled, hips rocking in the liana sling. "Your seed belongs only inside my body. Not on the ground."

Joey swallowed. "Yeah. Only inside you."

Tilting the blue bottle over Braeden's groin, Joey drizzled oil on his lover's cock and down the spread-open crease of his ass. He closed the bottle and let it fall to the ground, then pressed both thumbs against Braeden's entrance.

Braeden whimpered. "Ah, J-Joseph, yes, please, please."

"You're so beautiful," Joey whispered, and bent to kiss Braeden's knee. One thumb slipped into Braeden's hole, tearing a sharp cry from his lips and making his entire body shudder. "I love how you give yourself up to me when we fuck. You're always taking care of me,

Braeden. I love being able to take care of you for a change. To be able to give you this."

"You...you give me everything." Braeden gasped when Joey's other thumb slid in beside the first, both crooking to spread him open. "Oh. Joseph. Please fuck me now, my love, *a chuisle mo chroí,* fuck me, please!"

"Soon."

A swift thought brought more new tendrils shooting out of the thick vine supporting Braeden's hips. At Joey's command, they slithered between Braeden's legs, winding around his shaft and balls in a firm but gentle grip. Two soft green sprouts snaked into his open hole, caressing Joey's thumbs in passing. Braeden wailed, his cock pulsing under the onslaught.

Joey stared, panting. This was beyond all previous experience, beyond his wildest imaginings, and he could hardly believe he was the one making it happen. Making Braeden incoherent with pleasure. Braeden's white skin glowed in the light of the waxing gibbous moon, and his sharp cries rode the air. At Joey's feet, the grasses swayed from the frantic fluttering of Braeden's wings. Joey could smell the musk of Braeden's arousal, even over the scents of flowers, water and greenery, and two unwashed males.

The urge to wallow in that overwhelming, exciting aroma was too strong to resist, and Joey didn't want to try. Dropping to his knees with both thumbs still imbedded in Braeden's ass, he nuzzled Braeden's balls, rasping his unshaven cheek against the sensitive skin then licking it to soothe away the stubble burn. Braeden babbled in Gaelic, his voice hoarse and breathless. The constant movement of his body caused his hole to contract around Joey's thumbs and the slender vine tendrils. Joey wondered what it would feel like to have liana sprouts in his ass, caressing his insides and tickling the nerve-rich skin of his anus. *Gotta try that sometime,* he promised himself.

With one last swipe of his tongue around Braeden's opening, Joey rose to his feet, leaned over and kissed his lover's taut, sweat-dewed belly. "Are you ready?" he asked, removing the vines from Braeden's ass with a thought and poising his cockhead there.

Braeden just stared, his breath coming in shallow gasps, and Joey grinned. Braeden was normally a talker during sex. It wasn't often Joey could make him completely nonverbal. Taking it as an invitation, Joey bit his lip and sank his cock deep into Braeden's unresisting body.

"Oh, oh yes, yes-yes-yes," Braeden chanted, head lolling back and body arching. "Yes, fuck me, fuck me, oh Danu yes!"

"Yes," Joey echoed. He clamped his hands onto Braeden's hips to hold him still and plunged into him in short, hard strokes. "Fuck, that's good."

Braeden's grunts and moans seemed to agree. Responding to Joey's silent command, the vines around Braeden's cock gripped tighter, squeezing and stroking and kneading his balls in a rhythm to match Joey's thrusts. New tendrils whipped down from above, wound tiny shoots around Braeden's nipples and tugged hard. The flesh stretched tight, and Braeden whimpered, head thrashing.

Braeden's ass contracted around Joey's cock, and his vision blurred. "God, fuck, almost there," he gasped.

Braeden stared at Joey, wide eyes gleaming silver. A single thin liana sprout slipped into the slit in the tip of Braeden's cock, and he came with a scream that echoed in the night air. Semen splattered his chest and stomach, its pearlescence blending with his ghostly skin. The sight of Braeden covered in his own come, shuddering with the force of his orgasm, tipped Joey over the edge. He came deep in Braeden's ass, fingers gripping his hips with bruising force.

"Oh fuck." Joey managed to pull out before his knees buckled and he dropped to the ground. He leaned his dripping forehead against Braeden's butt and drew a deep breath. "Mm. You smell like sex."

A dazed laugh came from the direction of Braeden's head. "I imagine the smell of not bathing for three days is stronger."

"Not from this angle." Joey kissed one firm cheek, getting a smear of his own semen on his chin, then flopped onto his back. He thought out to the liana. They lowered Braeden gently to the ground, unwound themselves from him and hissed back into the darkness.

The moment Braeden was free, he rolled over and straddled Joey's body. The moonlight caught in his hair, creating a shining white curtain all around them. Smiling, Joey tilted his head to meet Braeden's kiss.

"You are quite a creative lover, *a chuisle.*" Braeden nuzzled Joey's cheek. "I have never had a vine inside me before."

"I don't know why I wanted to do that." Joey rubbed a thumb over one of Braeden's swollen nipples. "I thought it would be hot, and it was. But more than that, I liked that I *could* do it, you know? That I could have that kind of control over you." He glanced up at Braeden, wanting him to understand. "I never would've let them hurt you. I wouldn't have done it if I wasn't one hundred percent sure I could control them."

"I know." With one more brief press of lips, Braeden pulled back and sat up on his knees, wings shimmering in the moonlight. "What just happened was incredible, Joseph. And the level of control you exhibited over your magic proves to me that you are ready to face your father."

Something cold and hard curled in Joey's belly. "Hey, if you were thinking about business just now I must've been doing something wrong."

He was trying to keep his tone light, so Braeden wouldn't see the bitterness he still felt over what he had to do. As usual, though, Braeden saw right through him. Reaching over and grabbing Joey's hands, Braeden pulled him up and into a tight embrace.

"I know you are afraid," Braeden said, his breath stirring Joey's hair. "I know you don't want to do this. I'm sorry this burden falls to you. But I will be beside you, my love. I will do everything in my power to help you. And I will be there for you when it's over." He kissed Joey's temple, stroked his bare back. "You are strong, Joseph. Remember that."

Joey's throat constricted. He nodded against Braeden's shoulder. "Let's go get clean now."

"Very well." Drawing back, Braeden rose to his feet, then held down a hand to help Joey up.

They walked to the pool hand in hand. A few minutes later, they had enough soapberry seed pods ground up to wash with. Joey stood under the little waterfall and let the cool flow pound all thought out of him. Tomorrow, he could.face what was ahead. Right now, he just wanted to forget.

Chapter Eight

Braeden woke to the sound of a loud splash. He sat straight up, blinking in the morning light. The pallet of leaves and grasses was empty save for himself. Joseph was nowhere to be seen, either in the little shelter or immediately outside.

After a split second of bright terror, Braeden realized Joseph must have gone for a swim. He'd fallen in love with the little jungle pool the night before, declaring it his favorite place in the world and remaining in the water until Braeden forcibly removed him and ordered him to rest. Just like a child, Joseph had grumbled and complained, then fallen instantly asleep in Dracden's arms. Braeden hadn't minded. It was good to see the worried crease erased from Joseph's brow and his eyes shining with sheer carefree joy, even if it was only temporary.

Rising to his feet, Braeden conjured a new set of clothes for Joseph. Leaving them neatly folded beside the pallet, he wandered outside the shelter. The sun was already high in the sky, more than halfway to noon. Not that they had any agenda to follow. Joseph's control over his magic had become more finely tuned by the day, to the point where it was nearly subconscious. He'd gone beyond the need for practice. The previous night's encounter had proven that beyond any doubt.

The memory sent a rush of heat through Braeden's body. He'd never felt anything like the alien touch of the liana, animated by his lover's silent commands, Joseph's power thrumming through him like an electric current. Never had he felt more alive.

"Braeden."

At the sound of Joseph's voice, Braeden shook himself out of his thoughts. Shading his eyes with his hand, he squinted across the pool to where Joseph perched naked on a rock ledge beside the waterfall. "Good morning," he called, smiling. "Did you not get enough of the water last night?"

"Nope. I like it, thought I'd mentioned that." Joseph patted the flat space on the rock beside him. "Come over here."

Braeden obediently took wing and flew over to join Joseph. He settled on the sun-warmed rock, letting his wings trail over the edge behind him. "This is lovely," he sighed, tilting his face up to catch the cool spray from the waterfall. "Shall I gather us some breakfast? There are edible fish in this pool, and a variety of fruits, berries and roots growing in this area."

"I could eat, yeah." Joseph leaned over and kissed his shoulder, wet hair tickling his skin.

Braeden started to stand, so he could fly up to the jungle above the waterfall and find some food, but Joseph stopped him with a hand on his arm. A moment later, something rustled overhead. Braeden looked up and was startled to see two liana lowering a huge banyan leaf toward them. It sagged in the middle, as if weighted by something. Joseph carefully removed it from the liana's grip, and Braeden laughed in delight. The makeshift basket brimmed with papayas, plantains and bananas.

"You're beginning to think very creatively in regards to your magic, love," Braeden said, plucking a banana from the pile and stripping off the peel. "That was quite clever."

"Clever as last night?" Joseph picked up a papaya and took a big bite, eyes twinkling.

Braeden's cock twitched at the reminder. He hummed around a mouthful of banana. "My love," he said after he'd swallowed the fruit, "nothing could compare to last night in terms of creativity, or anything else."

Joseph grinned. "You looked unbelievably hot tied up with vines, you know."

"I rather enjoyed being completely in your power." Leaning over, Braeden licked a trickle of papaya juice from Joseph's chin. "When all this is over, we really must do it again."

Instantly, Joseph's body tensed. "I don't want to think about it."

"Of course not." Braeden tucked a lock of hair behind Joseph's ear. "But you must, love. Taking human transport rather than using magic will have thrown

Caratacus off long enough to let us reach this place and prepare for him, but he *will* find us. And when he does, we must be ready for him."

"I know that," Joseph snapped. "You don't have to keep reminding me, okay?"

Braeden managed to keep his countenance calm in spite of the ache in his heart. Very deliberately, he took another bite of banana, chewed and swallowed. "It is my duty to help you prepare for what you must face, Joseph. No matter how much either of us dislikes it. So yes, I do have to continue to remind you of what lies ahead and what must be done."

Sighing, Joseph stared at the partially eaten papaya in his hand. "I'm sorry, Braeden. I know you're right. That bastard Caratacus forced all this on me. On *us*. None of it's your fault, and I shouldn't yell at you about it."

"It's all right." Braeden stroked Joseph's hair, which was already beginning to dry in the tropical sun. "It's as you said. Caratacus forced us both to this pass. You never would have known of him, never mind set a goal to kill him, if he hadn't decided to take your life the moment the prophecy was spoken."

"Causing his own downfall by trying to change what's supposed to happen, just like you said before." Joseph took a bite of fruit, giving Braeden a curious look as he chewed. "I just realized something. You know everything there is to know about me, but I hardly know anything about you. You were a spy and a warrior in Tir-na-nog, and you're loyal to the real king. That's all I know about you."

Braeden's stomach knotted. He'd known this would come, eventually, but that didn't make it any easier to answer the questions Joseph would surely have. He tossed his banana peel on the ground, picked up a plantain and turned it between his fingers. "What would you like to know, love?"

Joseph fell silent, staring at the water while he finished off the papaya. Braeden waited. Overhead, a flock of tiny turquoise birds rose twittering from the trees. Closing his eyes, Braeden drew a deep breath of warm, humid air scented with wild orchids and damp earth. He tried not to think of what Joseph would say when he heard Braeden's story.

He will defeat Caratacus, he told himself, listening to the hypnotic sound of the flowing water. *It will happen, no matter how much he may hate me in a few moments. That is all that matters.*

If he could only convince his heart of that.

"Why are you doing this?" Joseph asked finally. "I mean yeah, I know you want to take Caratacus down and put the rightful king in power. But you had to know what following my mom to the human world might mean. So why did you do it? What's the real reason, Braeden?"

Opening his eyes, Braeden looked over at Joseph. He'd turned to face Braeden, one leg curled underneath him and the other dangling over the edge of the rock. A sudden breeze tugged a strand of wavy black hair across his face. He brushed it aside, his gaze holding Braeden's.

"I was a spy in Caratacus's home," Braeden said quietly, watching Joseph's face. "Queen Brigitta suspected him of plotting treason, so she sent me to infiltrate his estate. I presented myself as loyal and intelligent, but not clever enough to outthink him, and begged to be allowed to serve him as his page. My lineage is a noble one, but I gave up my titles when I was very young, in order to serve the Queen as a soldier and spy. I was given a false identity, so when Caratacus had me investigated he found nothing but the story which had been planted for him to find—that of a low-ranking soldier in the Queen's army who'd become disenchanted with service and desired power and luxury, things Caratacus could supposedly give me."

Joseph let out a sharp laugh. "Not very smart, is he? He really should've been suspicious of that."

"Yes, he should have," Braeden agreed. "Caratacus's greatest flaw, other than his brutality, is perhaps his arrogance. He cannot conceive of anyone being able to outwit him, or double-cross him. That arrogance allowed me to come very close to being part of his inner circle before the end."

Joseph didn't seem surprised. "I wondered. You said you were a spy, and you knew so much about him." He tossed the papaya core on the ground and leaned a hand on the ledge. "But that doesn't really answer my question."

Braeden took a deep breath and let it out in a slow, steady stream, steeling himself for what he had to say. "While in Caratacus's household, I learned of his plan to murder the Queen. At that time, he had not yet performed the blood binding. I could have assassinated him then, but I did not. I chose to report back to Queen Brigitta instead, and in doing so I sealed her fate. He bound his four most faithful followers by blood magic the night I left, walked into the castle and killed her the very next day."

Frowning, Joseph shook his head. "How could you have killed Caratacus? I know you said he keeps Tir-na-nog under his thumb with the power he gained through the blood magic, but he had to have been powerful to start with or he never could've taken over."

Braeden stared out over the pool, watching the sunlight glinting on the water. "He did not take the rule of Tir-na-nog through skill or finesse, or any particular strength in his innate magic. Before the blood binding, my own powers were as strong as his, and my gift for strategy has always been greater. My mistake lay in underestimating the depths to which he was willing to sink. I never thought he would cut himself off from the natural world—from all that is sacred to our kind—in order to gain powers dark enough to stain the very soul."

"So you think it's your fault he killed the Queen and took over the kingdom?" Joseph sounded faintly surprised. "Come on, Braeden, you have to know that's crazy."

"Is it? I had the opportunity and the ability to stop Caratacus before he performed the binding. I failed to act

147

on the opportunity. That failure cost the Queen her life, and cost every soul in Tir-na-nog their freedom. That is why I volunteered for this duty." Braeden turned and met Joseph's gaze. "I regret that my failure ultimately brought this burden upon you. But I do not regret taking this assignment, and I do not regret falling in love with you. And even though I have no right to ask it, I hope you will not regret what has happened between us either, now that you know the truth."

Joseph didn't speak, and Braeden held his breath. He would understand if Joseph wanted nothing to do with him now, and would accept it without argument. But it would still hurt worse than anything he'd ever experienced.

After a moment which lasted eons, Joseph took Braeden's hand, pulled him close and kissed him. "I don't regret it," Joseph whispered against Braeden's lips. "And as far as I'm concerned, you have nothing to prove and nothing to make up for."

Relief brought laughter bubbling up from Braeden's chest. He cupped Joseph's face in his hands, pressing their foreheads together. "I love you, *a chuisle.* So very much."

Joseph's answer wasn't in words, but it told Braeden everything he needed to know.

⁓

The remainder of the day was spent doing nothing but swimming, lying in the sun and talking of small matters. If Joseph had any further questions about Braeden's past, he didn't voice them. He seemed perfectly content with what he'd learned. There was no judgment in those dark eyes, no anger or resentment, and Braeden thanked the Goddess for that. It was more than he deserved, but he couldn't find it in him to question his good fortune, or to punish himself with further guilt. What had happened—and what had not—was in the past. Braeden vowed to himself that from this moment on, he would do his best to leave it there.

As the day drew to a close, they made love on the grass beside the stream, then lay together on the ground and watched the sunset bathe their secret hollow in a fiery glow. The trees formed a sharp black bas-relief against the red-orange sky. Somewhere in the depths of the jungle, an eerie cry rose and fell in an undulating wail which made Braeden's skin prickle. In that moment, he could have sworn they'd somehow been transported to the untamed lands on the outskirts of the Sidhe kingdom.

After a long, luxurious bath in the pool, in which Joseph insisted on washing not only Braeden's wings, but his hair as well, they settled in the little shelter for their night's rest. As before, Joseph was sound asleep in seconds. Braeden lay awake a while longer, trying without success to shake off a vague uneasiness which had been growing in him ever since darkness fell.

I am dreading the confrontation with Caratacus, he told himself, tightening his arms around Joseph's slumbering form. *We both are. Joseph is simply smart enough to cast his worry aside in order to rest while he can.*

Braeden smiled against Joseph's still-damp hair. He'd quickly learned that while Joseph wore his heart on his sleeve and had an impressive temper at times, he was one of the most practical human beings Braeden had ever met. He unerringly found the most efficient approach to nearly every situation, from putting together a meal to finding a path through a dense, uncharted forest. During their time in the jungle, he'd instinctively known to eat whenever they found food and rest when the opportunity presented itself, thus keeping his mind and body in the best possible condition.

You could learn a lesson, soldier. Chuckling quietly to himself, Braeden shut his eyes and forced himself to relax.

He'd just begun to drift off when a faint crackle sounded from outside the shelter. Frowning, Braeden carefully disentangled himself from Joseph's embrace and sat up. Whatever the noise was, it had come from the other side of the bamboo-and-banya-leaf wall not two feet to his right.

He stood and took a step forward, hoping it was simply some jungle animal he'd heard. Nocturnal creatures were plentiful here, and while a few could be dangerous under the right circumstances, most would not harm them except in self-defense. Centering himself, he stretched out his senses, feeling for any trace of magic.

He caught the dissipating energy of a recently closed portal into the Space just as Caratacus himself came into view around the wall of the shelter. His four unnamed followers hovered in midair behind him, faces blank as he drew on their power to fuel his own.

Braeden had a magical shield up before he consciously realized what he was seeing. "Joseph! Wake up."

Caratacus smiled, eyes glinting in the moonlight. He made a short, choppy motion with one hand, and Braeden's shield dissipated. Before Braeden could react, something hard, cold and heavy clamped onto both his wrists, holding his arms behind his back. A gag materialized around his mouth at the same time, thick cloth pressing between his lips and cutting into his tongue.

"Come," Caratacus said, as calmly as if he were taking Braeden to a social function at the castle. "We must go."

The last thing Braeden saw as Caratacus grabbed his arm and yanked him through another portal was Joseph's face, mouth stretched wide in a scream of anguish. Then the emptiness of the Space engulfed him and Joseph was gone.

Chapter Nine

The portal spit Braeden out in cool darkness. He landed on his knees on rough, icy stone. Somewhere behind him, firelight flared to life. Looking around, he saw he was in a cavern of some sort. The ceiling was low and uneven, and the walls were thick with shallow bays and narrow openings. A few of them curved off into blackness, hinting at an entire system of caves beyond this one. There was no moonlight showing from any of the openings, leaving him with no idea how far underground he was or which way was out.

The whisper of wings trailing on stone sounded to his left, and Caratacus glided into his line of vision, a wide smile on his face. His followers were nowhere in sight, but Braeden thought he could feel the dark taint of their magic in the shadows behind him.

"Welcome, traitor, to my temporary headquarters." Caratacus swept his arm outward. "Clever as you are, I am certain you will realize why I chose this place. Nothing grows here. Therefore, my misbegotten offspring cannot use his magic. Powerful he may be, but without his mindless minions he is nothing."

Braeden glared, wishing he could point out the irony of his kidnapper's words. A single arched eyebrow told him Caratacus recognized it, but didn't care.

As long as he has the unlimited power he craves, he does not care whether it is his own or stolen, Braeden thought bitterly. *May Danu damn him to the pit.*

Caratacus sauntered closer, one long, thin finger tapping his chin. "You must be wondering why I did not simply kill the brat where he lay. I could have, certainly. The boy was helpless. Meat for the taking." He leaned down to stare straight into Braeden's eyes. "It seems you are as useless at protecting the one you love as you were at protecting your Queen."

Braeden knew better than to show how deep those words cut. He held Caratacus's gaze without flinching. After a moment, Caratacus straightened up with a shrug. "Where was I? Oh yes, telling you why I did not gut your young lover as he slept. As much as it galls me to admit it, the boy has something I need."

Fear twisted in Braeden's stomach. *No. Goddess, no.*

"My son's power over the plant world is greater than any I've ever witnessed," Caratacus continued, pacing a slow path from one side of the small chamber to the other. "It is the one thing I lack. With it, I could make my control over all of Faerie absolute. Joseph's death would have given me greater power than any Sidhe has ever known, it is true, but binding him to me will make me a god. Danu herself will not dare to defy me."

Braeden closed his eyes and breathed deep. In the years since Queen Brigitta's death, he'd learned a lot about the blood binding. Accurate sources of information were difficult to find in the human world, but not impossible if one knew where to look. A voluntary binding was stronger, but consent was not required to perform the spell. Caratacus could bind Joseph against his will. All he had to do was lure him here.

He has brought me here as bait. Joseph will certainly come after me. And his fate will be far worse than that of my Queen. The knowledge made Braeden feel sick.

A brutal yank on his hair made Braeden's eyes fly open. He stared up into Caratacus's face, inches from his own, and nearly despaired at the mad gleam in those virulent green eyes.

"Your lot in this life is to be the agent of destruction for all you love," Caratacus growled. "I tell you all of this so that you may know what you have brought about, and suffer for it before you die. And die you shall. Slowly and painfully." He let go of Braeden's hair and stood straight, corpse-white wings fanning out behind him. "You may have noticed that I've bound you with iron. Even the cloth preventing you from speaking has iron shavings woven into it. Even though you failed to stop me from taking the throne of Tir-na-nog, you betrayed me, and that betrayal must be punished. Lord Caratacus does not forget, or forgive."

Braeden blinked, noticing for the first time the burning in his wrists, lips and cheeks. The iron would eat slowly into his skin. If it remained in contact with his body long enough, it would cause permanent scarring and possibly damage to the nerves. The lustful shine in Caratacus's eyes said that possibility took precedence over the metal's magic-dampening properties as the main reason he'd chosen iron restraints.

Braeden acknowledged the growing discomfort and the probability that he would end up with debilitating scars, then let it slip to the back of awareness. Joseph had no way of knowing Caratacus planned not to kill him, but to bind him with blood magic. When he arrived—as he most certainly would—he would need help. Braeden needed to be sharp and focused if he hoped to be of any use to Joseph when the time came. He couldn't help feeling pain or fear, but he could not afford to let either distract him.

Shaking his head, Caratacus bent to caress Braeden's cheek. "You are powerful, Braeden. You could have been great, if you had only given your loyalty to me. That chance is now in the past. I shall take your lover's power as my own, and with it I shall rule all the worlds. Watch, and suffer, then die knowing you could do nothing to stop it."

Ignoring Caratacus, Braeden let his consciousness shrink inward. He could still hear his tormentor, could still feel the stone beneath his knees and the iron biting into his skin, but it all faded to the periphery of experience. Inside his mind, he lay in the cool, springy grass of the little hollow, with Joseph naked in his arms. He could feel the ghost of Joseph's breath against his cheek, Joseph's lips soft and warm on his own as they kissed.

The memory was real enough to drive away the gnawing ache in his mouth and wrists, and the sharp bite of stone digging into his knees. With this to sustain him, he could wait patiently as long as he needed to.

ა

Joey stood in the shade of a banyan, a thick spirit vine around his waist, contemplating the sheer drop-off inches from the ends of his bare toes. Unlike the ravine he and Braeden had encountered—was it only two days ago?—this chasm was at least one hundred feet across. Not that it mattered. Joey wasn't crossing this one. His destination lay at the bottom, hidden by shadows even though the sun was almost directly overhead.

It hadn't taken him long to figure out that Caratacus didn't want to kill him after all. He would have been easy prey, lying asleep in a bamboo shelter open on one side. Clearly, Caratacus had found them much earlier—and much more easily—than Braeden had thought he would, and he had something in mind other than death for Joey. Something which evidently involved luring him into the location of Caratacus's choosing by kidnapping Braeden.

By opening himself to the strange mind of the jungle, Joey had learned that Caratacus and his minions hadn't all traveled to this place using the Space between worlds. Joey suspected Caratacus had used the Space to bring

Braeden so he wouldn't have a chance to escape, taking two of his people with him and leaving the other two to lead Joey here. Those two had made the short journey on foot, leaving a trail of dead and dying vegetation in their wake. The jungle's collective consciousness still reeled with the shock of their passing. Joey had tracked the two easily enough by following the sounds of suffering in his head as trees, vines and flowers were randomly scorched or uprooted. The jungle plants led him on a straight path to his destination, clearing the ground beneath his feet as he went and steadying him when he stumbled in the dark before the sun rose.

Joey leaned as far over the edge of the chasm as he dared, calculating the best descent. The vines here at the top weren't anywhere near long enough to lower him all the way to the bottom. However, various roots and vines sprouted at intervals from the earthen wall. He could climb down if he was careful, using the protruding roots as steps and the thicker vines as safety ropes. It would be slow going, but that didn't make any difference. Caratacus wouldn't attack him here.

According to the memories of the trees and grasses, the two faeries had vanished into a hole in the earth. From his perch on the edge of this deep, dry sinkhole, Joey could just make out a low opening in the wall on the other side. It was partially obscured by a veil of wild orchids, some of which had been torn down and trampled into the dirt.

Something told Joey those flowers would be the last growing things he encountered if he entered the yawning blackness beyond. Caratacus wouldn't be stupid enough to confront him anywhere except a place barren of all life. A place where Joey would be unable to use his powers. A place like this underground cavern.

He couldn't imagine what Caratacus had planned for him, but it made no difference. Braeden's life was in danger, and Joey was determined to save him. He hadn't come unprepared. Since Caratacus had gone to such trouble to see that Joey wouldn't have any plants around, he'd brought his own.

Let's just hope he doesn't search me, Joey thought, fingering the seeds in the pocket of the jeans Braeden had conjured for him the previous day. Without those seeds, he and Braeden were both dead.

"Standing here worrying isn't helping," he told himself sternly. "Get on with it."

Nodding, Joey sat on the edge of the gulf, turned around and slipped over the side, with the spirit vine still tight around him. After a moment's fumbling, his feet found purchase on a wide root curving out from the wall, and he began to climb down.

The descent was long, slow and harrowing. Without the various vines and roots leaping into action at his slightest thought, he would have fallen within the first few minutes. Even with the help of the various plants, it took great care and all his concentration to reach the bottom. Though he hadn't been able to see it from above, the walls of the depression were undercut in several spots, making it impossible to find a foothold.

Joey groaned in relief when his searching feet settled on solid earth. He sat on the cool, damp ground, letting the tension drain from his muscles. The air smelled of orchids and rotting leaves. It was noticeably cooler here, still and breathless. The silence rang in his ears. Instinct told him the unnatural quiet could be blamed on the Sidhe who'd led him here.

Forcing himself to focus, Joey looked around. The mouth of the cave lay almost directly across from where he sat. A single ray of sunshine slashed through the empty space between him and the cave, sparkling on bits of dust and dirt in the air, but no light fell on the aperture itself. It waited for him, black and forbidding.

It was the last place he wanted to go, but he had no choice. Braeden was in there, at the mercy of someone who wouldn't hesitate to hurt him if that's what it took to get Joey to enter that cave.

Using the earth wall behind him for support, Joey rose to his feet. He took a deep breath and let it out, then started toward the cave mouth. His legs trembled, and his heart pounded so hard he could hear it in his skull. He was about to face Caratacus, and that confrontation might very well result in death—or worse—for both himself and his lover. The knowledge terrified him.

It's okay to be afraid, he reminded himself as he paced across the thin grass, remembering what Braeden had told him over and over again in those two weeks in the North Carolina mountains, a lifetime ago. *Do not try to deny it, but do not let it rule you,* Braeden's voice echoed in his memory. *Acknowledge it, allow yourself to feel it, and*

159

let it go. Only then will you be able to do what must be done.

Repeating that mantra to himself, Joey moved the curtain of orchids aside with a gentle thought and entered the dense darkness beyond.

Once his eyes adjusted, he saw the distinctive flicker of firelight against the stone walls. A narrow passage sloped steeply downward. About fifty feet in, it curved to the right. The orange light came from beyond the curve.

Gathering his courage, Joey strode down the tunnel toward the light. When he rounded the bend, he saw a torch wedged into a crack in the cave wall. Its flame threw dancing light and looming shadows against the dark stone.

Taking the torch as he was clearly meant to do, Joey continued deeper into the cavern. The passageway eventually leveled off. The air grew cooler as he went, and he was soon glad he'd worn the jeans. He wished he'd taken the time to put on the T-shirt and sneakers too. The cold seeping up through the stone floor numbed his bare feet, and gooseflesh prickled his naked arms and chest.

Joey tried to keep track of how long he followed the pathway deeper into the earth. But with no watch and not even the slightest glimpse of the sky, he had no way of guessing. After a while, time ceased to have any meaning. He'd been walking forever, cold and scared and alone, with the weight of the planet above his head and the burden of its future on his shoulders.

When he heard the first sounds, he stopped in his tracks, heart racing. Soft grunts, low voices and a susurration like silk dragged over stone drifted to him from around a sharp bend in the passageway. It was obvious that he'd found Caratacus and his men, and hopefully Braeden as well.

Adrenaline sharpened his senses to razor keenness. He edged closer to the turn, listening as hard as he could. The sharp crack of leather on skin rang out, followed by a muffled cry and a harsh, cruel laugh.

"Please, come in, my son," Caratacus called, his voice mocking. "We have been waiting for you."

Joey's insides knotted. *This is it. Don't fuck this up.* He dropped the torch on the ground. Clenching his hands into fists so they wouldn't shake, he marched around the corner with his stride full of a confidence he didn't feel. The passageway opened into a small, low-ceilinged cavern lit by several torches in the walls. Joey stopped, forcing himself not to react to what he saw.

Braeden knelt in the middle of the floor, hands bound behind his back. A gag was tied across his mouth. The skin around the gag was red and swollen, and crimson spots speckled the cloth. Blood ran in rivulets from several slashes across his chest and abdomen. As Joey watched, horrified, Caratacus nodded to one of his followers, who lifted the whip in his hand and dealt Braeden a lashing blow across the fronts of his thighs. Braeden stiffened and let out a grunt behind the gag.

"Stop!" Joey cried before he could stop himself.

"But I am so enjoying seeing him suffer." Tilting his head, Caratacus gave Joey a questioning look. "Do you mean to say that the two of you have not explored the joys of pain together? You really must, you know. You are of my blood; you will find that binding your lover and inflicting pain upon him gives you immense pleasure."

A vision of Braeden wrapped in vines, immobilized with his legs spread, flashed into Joey's mind. He shoved it uneasily away. "What do you want? Why did you bring me here?"

"I want only what I told you before," Caratacus answered. "My son by my side."

"Bullshit," Joey spat. "You tried to kill me the day I was born. I know about the prophecy."

"It is true. I did seek to end your life before you could end mine. But that is no longer my goal." Caratacus spread his hands palms outward in a gesture of peace Joey knew to be utterly false. "Will you not rule along with me, Joseph? Together, we will be unstoppable. You will have everything your heart desires. Even Braeden, if you wish it."

Joey dared a hard look at Braeden. The silver-gray eyes were clear and focused, in spite of the pain Joey knew he must be feeling. He flicked his gaze down to Joey's jeans pockets and back up, and Joey knew he'd felt the presence of the seeds there. Joey did his best to put his understanding in his eyes. *I just have to make Caratacus think he's got me. Then we'll strike.* Braeden could get the seeds Joey carried where they needed to be. All Joey had to do then was make them grow.

Tearing his gaze from Braeden's, Joey stuck his hands in his pockets in what he hoped was a casual movement. "I won't have him enslaved, or killed. If I join you, you have to let him go free."

Caratacus arched one fine chestnut brow, green eyes glinting with a greedy light, and Joey knew he had him. Arrogance was Caratacus's flaw, not stupidity. He'd never have believed it if Joey agreed to join him without asking for Braeden's life in return. Not that Joey believed for a second Caratacus would actually let Braeden go. Not that it mattered, since Joey's plans most definitely didn't include joining Caratacus in his reign of brutality. Caratacus clearly thought Joey had a great deal of raw power, but no capacity for bold action, and Joey planned on using that to his advantage.

"Very well," Caratacus said. "If you will agree to join me, your lover will go free. However, he will not be allowed access to my court, or to you, as long as he walks free. Are you quite certain you do not want him bound as your slave?"

Joey gave a brusque nod. "I'm sure. I want him freed."

Caratacus's smile chilled Joey's blood. "Very well. It shall be done."

Yeah. Right. Good thing I'm not counting on that. "What do I do?" Joey asked, trying to keep his voice steady.

"I shall bind you to me with blood magic." With a strange twist of his long fingers, Caratacus summoned what Joey recognized as an iron knife with a silver handle from the other side of the room. "Do not think you can destroy me through that connection, Joseph. I am far too powerful."

The realization of just what Caratacus was doing hit Joey like a brick between the eyes. He swallowed. "What if you can't access my power over plants? What if the blood binding cancels that out? Will you still let Braeden go, if I stay with you?"

Caratacus shrugged, but the look in his eyes said if this didn't work, Joey and Braeden would both die. "That remains to be seen. Give me your dominant hand."

Joey gasped as an unseen force took hold of his right wrist and pulled. He closed his fist around the handful of seeds a split second before Caratacus's magic ripped his hand from his pocket. The invisible grip yanked Joey's arm out straight, the inside of his wrist offered up to the knife.

Caratacus took no notice of Joey's tightly clenched fingers. Holding the knife in one open palm, he moved his free hand over it, muttering something in Gaelic. Beside him, Braeden watched from behind a veil of hair. Joey could see the keen gleam of his eyes flicking between him and Caratacus, waiting for the right time. It made Joey feel calmer. Steadier. Like they could actually pull this off.

Whatever spell he'd used on the knife done, Caratacus shifted his hand to grip the handle. Joey caught a glimpse of reddened skin where the iron had lain healing in an instant, and his eyes widened.

Caratacus laughed, and gestured toward one of his followers, who stood silent against the wall. "Tuathal has the power of healing all wounds, even those inflicted by iron. Even wounds so severe they would be fatal to us regardless of whether iron was used. Did you not know? It is most useful." He stalked up to Joey, white wings fluttering behind him. The red veins looked black in the firelight. "Do not move, and do not fight me. If you do, Braeden dies."

Joey held still as Caratacus pressed the knife point into his own wrist and cut swiftly downward, uttering a sing-song incantation at the same time. Still chanting, he took hold of Joey's arm and laid the bloody knife tip to his wrist.

Joey's mind raced. The revelation that one of Caratacus's followers had healing powers above and beyond the accelerated healing all Sidhe were born with changed things. What if Caratacus could draw enough of the healing magic to save himself from the latent life Joey held in his palm? If that was the case, everyone in two worlds—possibly more—was doomed. If Joey waited just a moment, until the spell had begun to bind them, maybe he could reverse the power flow enough to let the seeds do their work.

It was a risk, but Joey felt in his gut it was worth taking. If he had no chance of making it work, why would Caratacus have felt threatened enough to warn him against trying it?

Holding his breath, Joey let Caratacus cut into his wrist. Instantly, he felt a tingle of magic move up his arm.

165

The blood flowing from the cut burned his skin. Still, he waited. The connection with Caratacus and his men needed to be established.

He felt Braeden's agitation as Caratacus moved his own bleeding arm over Joey's. *Just another second,* Joey thought, watching his father's arm lower toward his. *Just until I feel it...*

Staring at Joey with triumph in his eyes, Caratacus pressed their bleeding wrists together. A pulse of magic surged through Joey's body, strong enough to blur his vision and tear a cry from his throat. Braeden let out a strangled shout. Joey opened his hand and felt Braeden's power crackle across his palm.

Caratacus's eyes went wide as a cloud of seeds flew from Joey's palm into his nose and throat, guided by Braeden's magic. He coughed, but it was too late. Bits of green were already sprouting from his mouth, packing months and years of growth into seconds at Joey's command.

"Stupid child," Caratacus choked. A bright green tendril snaked from his mouth to wind around his neck, cutting off his words. He grasped at the vine with both hands, the knife clattering to the floor.

Through the fragile connection between himself and Caratacus, Joey felt his father's mind reach out to Tuathal, the healer. Tuathal's eyes glazed white, his face slack as his master drew on his magic.

Now, Joey told himself. *Do it now.*

Focusing on the magic binding him to Caratacus, Joey felt along their connection, to Caratacus and beyond. After a moment's fumbling, he grasped the thread of power and pulled it into himself.

Instantly, the cut on Joey's wrist knitted together, sending a fierce burning sensation up his arm. Caratacus gurgled and fell to his knees. Tiny branches punched through his eyes and cheeks, sending a spray of blood across the floor from their unfolding leaves as they grew. The droplets burned where they spattered Joey's feet.

With a final sigh, Caratacus went limp, his body held upright by the tree whose roots pierced his belly and groin to tear through the solid stone below. The branches lifted toward the ceiling, seeking the sun. Liana and orchids wound around the wooden limbs.

Joey stared, stunned by what he'd done. An icy lump formed in his gut.

"Joseph? Are you all right, love?"

Joey's head snapped up, seeking his lover. Braeden stood with both palms out, holding Caratacus's four disciples against the wall with a shield of shimmering magic. All four cowered before Braeden's power. Joey's partially formed bond with Caratacus had created a weak connection with his followers as well. It was already starting to fade, but was still strong enough for Joey to feel their weakness and fear. He wondered what had weakened them so much, but not enough to spare any thought on the matter. Not when Braeden was free of his bonds and their goal was accomplished.

"How'd you get loose?" he asked, glancing at the open shackles and torn gag on the ground. "I'm glad you did, but how?"

"My bonds were held in place by magic," Braeden explained. "I was able to remove them when Caratacus died." He shot Joey an indecipherable look. "He bound me with iron. Had you not lured him so close to you, I could not have forced those seeds into him."

Joey felt the blood drain from his face. Iron dampened Sidhe magic, and was one of the few things that could kill or permanently damage them. "Christ."

"Yes. But let us not think of what *could* have happened. He is defeated. That is what is important."

"Yeah. You're right." Thinking out to the vines still growing from Caratacus's body, Joey sent thick ropes of liana over to bind the four Braeden held captive. Wads of leaves stuffed themselves into the faeries' mouths, preventing them from speaking any spells. "You can let them go now. I've got them."

Braeden let the magic shield drop. His shoulders drooped, his wings sagging behind him. He drew a deep, shaking breath and pushed trembling hands through his hair. Joey gasped when he saw the raw, weeping flesh of Braeden's wrists.

"Shit, Braeden. Your wrists." Joey bounded over to take Braeden's hands in his. He winced at the sight of the ruined skin, leaking blood and serous fluid. "What did he do?"

"The cuffs were iron, as I've said. There was iron in the cloth he gagged me with as well, and in the leather of the whip."

Joey lifted his gaze to Braeden's face. "Oh my God," he exclaimed, taking in the livid red marks on Braeden's cheeks and the blisters on his lips. "Will it heal?"

"The burns will heal, yes, but they will leave permanent scars." Braeden gave him a sad smile. "At least there is no damage to the nerves. You arrived in time to prevent that."

"I'm sorry, Braeden." Burying his hands in Braeden's hair, Joey brushed their lips together in the tenderest of kisses. His chest tightened when Braeden tensed at the touch.

A flare of dark pleasure licked along the fading connection between Joey and the four Sidhe bound against the wall. One of them was evidently enjoying Braeden's suffering. Anger surged through Joey. Whirling around, he pinned the faery with a deadly glare. But before he could say anything, an idea stopped him cold.

Turning to face Braeden's questioning expression, Joey reached up and laid his palms on Braeden's cheeks, thumbs brushing his swollen lips. "Hold still. I want to try something."

Reaching along the rapidly weakening bond, Joey drew a thread of healing magic from Tuathal and thrust it into Braeden.

"Oh." Braeden gasped as the pulse of power hit him. In a heartbeat, the raw burns on his lips and cheeks melted into smooth, perfect skin. A swift swipe of a thumb healed the line of blisters on his tongue as well. "Joseph, what are you doing?"

Joey didn't answer. The connection with Tuathal was almost gone. He would have to work fast. Grasping Braeden's wrists and ignoring his lover's hiss of pain, he sent another wave of magic into him. This one was weaker, but he managed to get the skin to knit over the open wounds before the bond broke for good.

Braeden caught him when his knees buckled and lowered them both carefully to the floor. Cupping Joey's face in one palm, Braeden kissed his lips.

"Thank you," Braeden said, his breath warm and sweet against Joey's mouth. "You have quite a quick mind, my love."

Joey pressed as close as he could without putting pressure on the bleeding whip marks covering the front of Braeden's body. "I'm sorry I couldn't heal it all."

"The burns on my face and mouth were the most painful, and those are gone now. The iron in the whip was not in contact with my skin long enough to cause lasting damage. The cuts should heal well, with little if any scarring." Laying a hand on Joey's cheek, Braeden smiled. "You overcame the greatest threat the worlds have faced in many lifetimes, and you had the presence of mind to use a fast-fading blood bond to heal my wounds. Never think that you did not do enough. You have done more than should be expected of anyone."

Joey rested his head on Braeden's shoulder, one hand slipping around his waist to stroke his wing. "What do we do with the others?"

"I'm not certain." Braeden frowned. "They should be returned to Tir-na-nog. But I do not know how we are to send them there."

"We can't just take them?"

"You know that the stream of time flows differently in the world of the Sidhe than it does here. If we go there now, we have no way of knowing how much time will pass here while we are gone."

Joey stared into Braeden's eyes as the implications hit him. "Oh. Shit."

"Yes." Sighing, Braeden pulled out of Joey's arms and walked toward the wall where the four faeries lay bound by vines on the floor. "I wonder if we could— Oh, Danu."

"What?" Joey turned around, trying not to look at the grisly sight of Caratacus impaled on a tree. When he saw the four followers, his stomach plummeted into his feet. They lay silent and unmoving, unblinking eyes fixed on nothing. "Fuck."

"You did not kill them," Braeden said, reaching for Joey's hand as he moved to stand next to him.

"How do you know that?" Joey laced his fingers through Braeden's, swallowing against the nausea rising in his throat.

"They were bound to him by blood magic for many years. Their life-forces were inextricably woven through his. When he died, the sudden loss of his power was too much for them survive." Lifting Joey's hand, Braeden kissed his knuckles. "Their blood is not on your hands, *a chuisle*, though the blood of many innocents stains their own."

Joey didn't answer. Maybe these four had deserved to die many times over for the things they'd done. Caratacus had deserved to die if ever anyone had. But that didn't make the weight of five deaths any easier to carry.

"Can we go now?" Joey said, not even trying to fight the quaver in his voice. "We need to clean those cuts you have, then we both need to rest."

"Of course." Raising Joey's face with a finger beneath his chin, Braeden laid a soft kiss to his lips. "Shall we provide our green friends with sunlight and free air?"

"You can do that?"

"I believe so." Braeden tilted his head back to study the ceiling, then the wall on the other side of the chamber. "There is no more than six feet of rock above us, and a small clearing just on the other side of that wall. I can break up the rock with a pulse of power. Your tree's roots have already tapped deep, into the soil and groundwater below this cave. Our fallen enemies will provide further nourishment."

A few lilting Gaelic words and a strange twisting gesture from Braeden turned the stone roof above them into a rain of fine sand. Braeden sent it whirling away into piles against the walls. Sunlight poured in, painfully bright after the darkness of the cave. The torches flickered and died as sand and breeze hit them.

Joey glanced at the tree. The trunk was almost as thick as his waist. Caratacus's torso encased it like a horrific coat, long legs splayed out at unnatural angles on either side. As Joey watched, the tree trunk visibly expanded. Caratacus's ribs separated with a wet tearing sound, and his body fell in ragged halves on either side of the tree. One white wing stuck to the bark, gore dripping down the wood. The blood shone like wet paint in the sunlight.

A wave of dizziness washed over Joey. Bile rose in his throat. Stumbling across the room, he fell to his knees and vomited.

He didn't hear Braeden approach over the sound of his stomach emptying itself, but there Braeden was beside him, holding his hair away from his face, stroking his brow with a cool hand, whispering soft Gaelic endearments in his ear. When the spasms in his stomach eased and he could breathe again, Joey leaned into Braeden's strong arms and cried.

"It's all right, love," Braeden soothed, raking his fingers through Joey's hair. "You had no choice. I know that doesn't make it any easier, but it's true nevertheless." He kissed Joey's brow, wings folding around his body. "Let's leave this place, my love. Let the jungle take their bodies, and allow them the redemption of returning to the earth."

Joey nodded against Braeden's neck. "I want to go home, Braeden."

In the heartbeat of silence that followed, Joey knew what Braeden was thinking. The same thing he himself was thinking. That Braeden needed to return to Tir-na-nog. To bring the news that Caratacus was gone, and return the rightful king to the throne. To put a well-deserved end to his exile. Joey knew all of that. But he wasn't ready to let Braeden go, or to leave his home behind. So he nuzzled into Braeden's neck, breathing in his scent, and kept his thoughts to himself.

"Very well," Braeden said, his voice gentle. He rose to his feet, pulling Joey up with an arm around his waist. "Come, love. Hold on to me."

Joey slipped his arms around Braeden, rested his head on Braeden's shoulder and shut his eyes. When he felt the pull of the portal in the pit of his stomach, he welcomed it.

Chapter Ten

Braeden took them to the secret shelter first, to retrieve the knife which was all he had left of his family's ancient treasures. The other knives, the iron one and the silver ones Joseph had trained with, were most likely lost. Braeden didn't mourn them. Such weapons were easy enough to come by, if one knew where to go.

Joseph took some of the crushed soapberry and washed his hands and arms, then cleaned his teeth and tongue with leaves from a small plant Braeden recognized as a type of mint. Through the whole process, Joseph said not a word. Braeden didn't force the issue. After nearly four centuries, he still remembered his first kill. He'd scrubbed his hands until they'd bled.

In time, Joseph would come to terms with what he'd been forced to do. Meanwhile, Braeden's role was to offer him unwavering love and support. Sometimes silence accomplished that goal better than speech.

The heirloom knife in his possession once again, Braeden took Joseph through the Space between worlds to his mother's house. The place seemed empty and sad without Evangeline there.

"Sit down, love," Braeden instructed, pushing Joseph gently into a chair on the front porch. "Shall I open the door by magical means, or do you know where we might find a key?"

"There's one under the frog," Joseph answered, gesturing toward a large ceramic frog crouched beneath a day lily to the right of the porch steps. He glanced at the darkening sky as a rumble of thunder shook the air. "There's a storm coming. Let's stay out here for a little while and watch it." He frowned at the whip marks on Braeden's chest, belly and thighs. "Or maybe we should go in first and get those cleaned up."

"It can wait, love. I'd like to watch the storm myself, actually. I've always been fond of them."

Joseph still looked unsure. "I don't know. I don't want those cuts to get infected."

"They won't, never fear. See, they are no longer bleeding, and the skin has begun to knit." Braeden thumbed the edge of one cut, which still burned a bit but indeed had begun to close already. The iron shavings in the leather hadn't been enough to stop his body's accelerated healing processes. "I'll put on a glamour, and we shall watch the storm together."

Joseph's hand on his arm stopped him. One corner of Joseph's mouth curved up in a sad little half-smile at Braeden's questioning look. "The closest neighbors are two miles away, and you can't see the house from the road. Stay like you are."

"Very well." Glancing around, Braeden cast a surreptitious concealment spell around the entire area. To casual eyes, he and Joseph would be unseen. Feeling a bit more secure, he walked over to lean on the porch railing, gazing up at the glowering black clouds. "This is a lovely place. So peaceful."

"Yeah, it is." Behind Braeden, the chair creaked. He heard bare feet shuffling across wood, then Joseph's warmth pressed against his side. "That big oak's hollow. The one next to the driveway. I used to climb down inside it and pretend I was talking to it."

Braeden smiled. "Perhaps it was not pretend."

"Maybe not." Joseph slipped an arm around Braeden's waist. He was quiet for a moment, watching the tree branches toss in the rising wind. When he spoke, his voice was soft but defiant. "I'm not sorry. For any of it."

"Nor should you be," Braeden answered, laying his hand over his lover's where it rested on his hip.

They lapsed into comfortable silence. Lightning flashed vivid white across the black clouds. A heartbeat later, thunder rolled loud enough to rattle the old screen door in its frame. The air turned sharp and musky with the smell of oncoming rain. A fat drop hit an azalea leaf with a splat. Another clinked against the ceramic frog's head. Half a second later, the patter increased to a deluge and Evangeline's front yard was lost in a gauzy gray veil of falling water.

Leaning his head against Joseph's, Braeden closed his eyes and let the sound of the rain on the porch roof soothe him. Joseph faced a difficult decision in the days ahead, and his choice would have tremendous impact on Braeden's life. But with his love beside him and the cool, damp breeze rich with the sounds and smells of a stormy summer afternoon, such worries seemed part of a distant and hazy future. For now, he would set his troubles aside and simply savor the perfection of the present.

The loss of Joseph's warmth from his side was an unpleasant surprise. He opened his eyes just in time to see Joseph kick his blood-stained jeans aside and bound down the steps into the rain. Standing naked in the middle of the path, he spread his arms wide and tipped his face up to the sky. The curling ends of his rain-soaked hair brushed the swell of his ass.

"Joseph?" Braeden called, moving to stand at the bottom of the steps. "What are you doing?"

Joseph turned, a smile curving his lips. "I used to love playing in the rain."

"It seems you still do," Braeden answered, smiling in return.

Striding over to him, Joseph held a hand out in invitation. "Come out here with me."

Braeden laid his hand in Joseph's and let the man lead him into the storm. The rain was a chill shock, the drops pounding his skin and his wings in a prickling staccato rhythm. Joseph's body pressed to his, hands sliding around to stroke the spot where his wings sprang from his back. The cuts crisscrossing the front of his body stung from the water and the press of Joseph's skin against his, but the discomfort didn't stand a chance against the need rising through him like a tide.

Judging by the feral gleam in Joseph's eyes, the same fire burned inside him. "Fuck me," Joseph murmured, brushing his lips against Braeden's jaw. "Right here, outside in the rain. Fuck me."

The words made Braeden's knees weak. Groaning, he lifted his chin for more of Joseph's kisses and quick, sharp bites. "You...you wish me to have you thus?"

"Mm-hm." Joseph gazed up at him through half-closed eyelids, rainwater dripping from his parted lips and running in torrents down his neck and chest. "You've never been inside me, Braeden. Don't you want it?"

"Oh Danu yes," Braeden breathed, heart pounding. "I want you. Always, in every possible way."

Joseph hummed, one hand reaching between Braeden's legs to fist his cock. "Say it."

"Wh-What?" The feel of Joseph's fingers on him, peeling back his foreskin and rubbing a firm thumb across his slit, was rapidly eroding his ability to think.

"Tell me you want to fuck me." Cool, dripping fingers traced the flared head of Braeden's cock. "Tell me you want to ram this fat cock up my ass and pound me into next week."

Braeden's legs trembled. Despite centuries of life and more lovers than he could count, no one had ever affected him the way this young half-human, half-fae did. Joseph, with his unabashed sensuality and brazen way of speaking, made Braeden feel like a blushing virgin.

Because you are indeed a virgin in matters of the heart. Because for all the men you've bedded, you've loved none, until now.

He was just beginning to understand what a difference that made.

Sliding both palms down Joseph's rain-slick skin, Braeden grabbed his butt and squeezed hard. "I want to fuck you," he said, staring straight into Joseph's eyes. "I want to press you against a tree, sheathe my cock deep inside your beautiful body and, as you say, pound you into next week." He let out a breathless laugh. "Such strange things humans say to one another in the throes of passion."

"Maybe." Nuzzling his face into Braeden's neck, Joseph mouthed the point of his jaw. "But I love it when you talk dirty. Makes me so fucking hard for you."

"As I am for you, my love." Braeden thrust his hips forward so his cock slid wonderfully against Joseph's palm. The water running down their bodies squelched between them as their bellies pressed together, making them both laugh.

Taking Joseph's hands, Braeden pulled him toward the relative shelter of the nearby trees. The intertwining leaves overhead reduced the rain to a gentle sprinkle. A flash of lightning lit the sky, glinting on the puddles in the grass. The thunder that followed was further away than before, the storm rumbling its way north.

In the cool green gloom, Joseph fisted both hands in Braeden's hair and kissed him hard, tongue rough and demanding. He broke it just as suddenly as he'd begun it, turned around and braced his hands on a thick oak trunk. He shot Braeden a smoldering look over his shoulder.

Words weren't needed; Braeden knew what his Joseph wanted, and he intended to give it to him. Silently summoning the little bottle of oil, Braeden poured a good amount into his hand and let the bottle fall to the ground. He molded his body to Joseph's back, resting his cheek against the dripping black hair. Two of his fingers found Joseph's sweet hole and pushed inside. Strong muscles clutched his fingers tight.

Joseph shuddered, hands curling against the tree bark. "Fuck yeah. So good." He pressed his ass back, forcing Braeden's fingers in as deep as they would go, and let out a low moan. "God. Now. Now."

Yes. Yes, my love, my heart. Anything you wish. The words wouldn't emerge past the need clogging Braeden's throat, but he knew Joseph understood. Removing his fingers with as much care as he could, Braeden held Joseph's hole open with his thumbs and slid his cock inside.

Snug silken heat clutched him, and he had to fight the urge to come right then. He held still, panting into Joseph's hair, trying to regain his control. He didn't want to come yet. Not so soon. Joseph's body was a thing of boundless wonder, and he wanted to spend hours sheathed inside, just soaking up the feel of him.

Joseph whimpered and pushed back against Braeden's hips, wriggling in a way that almost undid him. "God, move already."

Hoping he could hold out at least a few minutes against the insistent ripple of Joseph's insides, Braeden slid back until only the head of his prick remained in Joseph's hole, then plunged back in with agonizing slowness. He watched his pale, rose-flushed cock disappearing between his lover's dusky cheeks and thought it was one of the loveliest sights he'd ever witnessed.

The tip of Braeden's cock brushed the slight firmness of Joseph's gland, and Joseph let out a sharp cry. "Fuck! Yes, fuck, do it. Fuck me."

The raw lust in Joseph's voice snapped the last thread of Braeden's control. Planting one hand on the tree trunk beside Joseph's and winding the other around his hips, Braeden did as Joseph asked.

The constant percussion of rain on leaves nearly drowned out Joseph's sharp little gasps, but Braeden heard them just fine. They fanned his arousal to a white-hot flame, tearing a string of Gaelic curses from his throat and speeding the rhythm of his pistoning hips until Joseph's body rocked forward with every stroke.

Braeden let his gaze slide up and down Joseph's body, drinking in the sight of him. Long hair clung in wet clumps to his face and arms, and spilled over his shoulders to swing between his chest and the tree. Rainwater traced winding rivers down his back and trickled over his ass to flow over the curves of strong muscle in his thighs. His skin felt feverish against Braeden's palm, in spite of the rain.

"*Tá tú go h-álainn, a chuisle,*" Braeden whispered, the words broken and breathless with the rhythm of their lovemaking. *Fucking,* Joseph would call it, and make them both harder than stone as a result. "So beautiful. So perfect." He took Joseph's prick in his hand, and it jumped and quivered at the touch. "Mine. Only mine, forever."

The possessive growl in his voice shocked him, but Joseph didn't seem to mind. Turning his head, he arched back to claim a hard kiss from Braeden. "Yours," he breathed into Braeden's mouth, one hand reaching back to tangle in his hair. "Always."

Joseph's words tightened Braeden's throat. Folding his wings around Joseph, Braeden devoured his mouth, the kiss all tongues and teeth and bruising lips. His hips slammed his prick into Joseph's body hard and fast, over and over again until he felt he might burst. Pre-come and the gentle rain shower eased the movement of his hand on Joseph's cock, and Joseph trembled against him.

His balls drew up hard and tight, his shaft swelling in Joseph's ass. His legs began to shake as the orgasm uncoiled like a great serpent in his belly. He came with a kiss-muffled shout, his wings quivering.

When the living grip of Joseph's insides had wrung the last pulse of pleasure from him, Braeden pulled out, kissed the corner of Joseph's mouth and sank to his knees in the wet grass. Weak and gasping with the force of his release, he leaned his forehead against the small of Joseph's back, hands caressing his lover's wet thighs. The smells of sweat, rain and sex made his head spin.

Whimpering, Joseph wriggled his backside against Braeden's throat. "Braeden, please," he begged. "So close, c'mon."

Braeden smiled, slid a finger into Joseph's wet, sticky crease, and circled his loosened hole. The muscles rippled and clenched at the touch, and Joseph moaned. "Never fear, my love. I will not leave you wanting."

Capturing a drop of semen as it dripped from Joseph's opening, Braeden used it to draw a shimmering heart on Joseph's right buttock. Smiling at his own actions, he grasped Joseph's hips and turned him around to lean against the tree trunk. Joseph stared down at him with unfocused eyes. Holding his gaze, Braeden leaned in and swallowed his cock to the root.

Joseph let out a wail. His head fell back against the tree trunk and his hips arched away from it, nudging the head of his prick against the back of Braeden's throat. Braeden hummed and swallowed, tearing another tortured cry from his love. He closed his eyes and began to move his head in a relentless rhythm intended to bring a man straight to the brink. Joseph's cock pulsed in his mouth, pre-come leaking bursts of rich male flavor on his tongue.

Beneath his knees, the thin grass rose around his thighs, undulating in response to Joseph's arousal. The branches overhead hissed with a movement no wind could produce, and he knew the tree also felt the echo of Joseph's pleasure. He could smell Joseph's excitement, mixed with the musky aroma of his own come running down the man's thighs. It was intoxicating, nearly as much as Joseph's sweet cries and broken declarations of undying love.

"Ohfuckohfuck," Joseph gasped, fingers grasping painfully at Braeden's hair. "Coming. Fuck, coming..."

Oh yes. Yes, love, yes. Braeden opened his eyes just as the first spurts of semen hit his tongue. The sun chose that moment to break through the tattered clouds and bathe Joseph in a golden light. Braeden swallowed the sweet-salty fluid, never once looking away from Joseph's face. Eyes screwed shut with pleasure, bare skin gleaming wet in the sunshine, mouth open in a soft litany of *ah-ah-ah* sounds, Joseph resembled more than ever a wild young god. Braeden felt privileged to kneel at his feet and suckle the warm seed fresh from his body.

He stayed there, stroking Joseph's softening cock with his tongue, until Joseph squirmed and pushed him away. "Sensitive," Joseph panted. He dropped to his knees and leaned against Braeden's chest. "I think you killed me."

Braeden smiled, petting his hair. "Somehow, I do not think so."

"But I can't move." Joseph plopped onto his back in the wet grass and gazed up at Braeden with sex-sated eyes. "Don't think I can go again today. You wore me out."

Laughing, Braeden leaned over and kissed Joseph's lips. "If there's one thing I have learned about you in these past weeks, Joseph, it's that you have an impressive amount of energy when it comes to lovemaking. I foresee that you will indeed 'go again' this day."

"Or *come* again, anyway." Joseph's lips curved into a teasing smile. "I'll just lie here and make you suck me off until I can't get it up anymore."

Unable to think of a single reason not to do exactly that, Braeden nodded, cupped Joseph's head in one hand and took his mouth in a deep, lazy kiss. Joseph opened to him with a breathy sigh. Strands of sodden black hair tangled into their mouths and clung to their faces. The rain had all but stopped, but a gust of wind shook a shower of cold droplets from the tree above onto Braeden's wings and back. He jumped when one fat drop ran down the crease of his ass, trickling cold and wet over his hole. Joseph laughed.

"Shall we go inside now, love?" Braeden brushed the hair from Joseph's flushed face. "You'll want to call your mother, I know." He was surprised, actually, that Joseph hadn't wanted to do so immediately, but he hadn't said anything about it. Long experience had taught him that a trauma such as Joseph had just been through often made one act in unexpected ways.

"I guess so." Joseph wound a strand of Braeden's soaked and tangled hair around his finger. "I want to talk to her, yeah, but…"

He trailed off, dark eyes sad and thoughtful. Braeden brushed a thumb across his cheek. "But what, *a chuisle*?"

Joseph remained silent. Braeden waited. When Joseph finally spoke, his voice was shaky and uncertain. "Once I call her, once she comes home, this'll all be over. And I'm glad the...the bad part's over now. That Caratacus is gone, but..." His breath hitched, lower lip trembling. "When we get up and go inside, this'll be over. And I don't want it to be."

Braeden felt as if a great hand had taken hold of his heart and squeezed. He knew his duty to his people. But he could find another way to carry it out, if need be. After all the sacrifices Joseph had made to save both the faery and the human worlds, didn't he deserve happiness? In that moment, Braeden knew he'd gladly bide for all time in the human world if it meant seeing his Joseph smile.

Stretching himself out on the grass beside Joseph, he gathered the man in his arms and held him tight. "It doesn't have to end, my love." He stroked Joseph's back, over and over in a comforting rhythm. "There are choices that must be made, by both of us. But I would sooner die than lose you now."

Joseph didn't answer, but his strangled sob and the tightening of his arm around Braeden's neck spoke volumes.

They lay tangled together on the ground beneath the trees for a long while. By the time Joseph unwound himself from Braeden's arms and stood, the clouds had scattered and the afternoon sun had nearly dried the damp from the grass. Braeden took the hand Joseph offered and rose to his feet.

"Are you ready, love?" he asked, lacing his fingers through Joseph's.

"Yeah." Joseph chewed his bottom lip, brows drawing together in thought. "Let's clean those cuts first, then I'll call Mama."

"Very well." Pulling Joseph close, Braeden kissed his forehead. "I will never desert you, Joseph. Not for any reason. This is my vow to you."

Joseph's smile was sad, in spite of the love shining in his eyes. "I know what you have to do as well as you do, Braeden. Don't make vows you might be forced to break." Drawing out of Braeden's embrace, Joseph tugged on his hand. "Now come on. We have things to do."

Having no idea what to say, Braeden followed Joseph in silence. Evangeline's day lilies, battered by the hard rain, perked their leaves and burst into bloom at a quiet word from Joseph as he fetched the house key from beneath the ceramic frog in the garden. Braeden wished he had the power to take the bitter sorrow from Joseph's eyes and replace it with the untainted happiness he so deserved.

If I leave, he will mourn me as I will mourn him, and I cannot bear being the cause of his unhappiness, Braeden mused while Joseph unlocked the front door. *Yet if I stay, he will never be content, because he will know I sacrificed my home and my duty to remain by his side. What then is the answer?*

There was, he knew, only one other option. For Braeden, it was a dangerously seductive one, because he himself would have all his heart's desire. But Joseph would have to give up everything he knew and loved.

I cannot ask it of him, Braeden decided, following Joseph into the house. *He has sacrificed too much already.*

Which left them back at the beginning of a circular argument, with no answer in sight.

When Joseph came into his arms with soft caresses and warm, sweet kisses, Braeden let the weight of the future slide from his shoulders. They could work out some sort of solution. They had to. Braeden had no intention of letting Joseph go, and he knew Joseph felt the same.

Casting his worry aside once again, Braeden closed his eyes and let himself fall into Joseph's kiss.

(℅

Joey's mother arrived the next evening, just before sunset. As soon as he saw the car coming up the drive, Joey jumped up from the chair on the front porch where he'd been waiting.

"She's here," he called over his shoulder through the open window. "Come on."

He bounded down the front steps, not waiting to see if Braeden would follow. Something told him Braeden would remain inside, to give him and his mother a few minutes alone. Braeden had spent the last couple of hours tidying the house and fixing dinner, mostly by hand though he'd used his magic now and then to make the process easier. Joey had started out with every intention of helping, but after the fourth time he'd dashed to the front window thinking he'd heard his mother's car, Braeden had ordered him to go out to the porch and wait.

He's so good to me, Joey reflected as the old station wagon rolled to a stop. *I love him so much. I don't want to lose him.*

Just the thought of being without Braeden made him feel sick. Shaking it off, he ran over to the driver's side door and scooped his mother into a tight embrace as she emerged from the car.

"Hi, Mama," he said, kissing her cheek. "I missed you."

"I missed you too, baby." Mama drew back, holding him at arm's length and giving him a thorough once-over. "I know you said on the phone you were all right. But are you, really? Did he hurt you?"

"I'm fine." Joey grinned at her, hoping she wouldn't see the complex tangle of emotions snarled in his brain. "I'll get your bags and we'll go inside. Braeden's making dinner."

She chuckled. "Now there's a picture. A faery cooking."

"He's a good cook. I guess he learned from being in our world for so long."

"I expect so." She pinned him with a sharp look. "Maybe it's none of my business, but you look like something's bothering you. Something big. You want to talk about it?"

Joey dropped his gaze to the ground. "It's complicated, Mama."

She laughed, the sound soft and humorless. "Baby, I was kidnapped from my home when I was sixteen and taken to a world I had no idea existed until then. I spent several years as a prisoner in a gilded cage, and when I finally escaped I spent the rest of my life 'til now terrified of them finding us. You are the one thing in my life that's purely good, and nothing about you has ever been simple. I think I know a little something about complicated problems."

Surprised, Joey met his mother's gaze. Her eyes were full of sympathy and the ever-present desire to help. Taking her hands in his, he smiled. "Yeah, I guess you do."

She squeezed his fingers. "You want to talk privately, or you want Braeden involved? I got a feeling this concerns him, but if you want to keep it between you and me we can do that."

Joey considered. "No. You're right, it does concern him, and he needs to be involved in the discussion. We haven't really talked about it yet. We have to, I know, but it's just...it's hard, you know?"

"Yes, I know." Shaking her head, Mama let go of Joey's hands and went to open the back door. "You men, always avoiding what's got to be done."

Joey started to protest that he hadn't avoided anything, had in fact faced a truly terrible duty head-on. He stopped when he saw his mother's face. The light in her eyes showed she understood exactly how much Joey had faced in the past weeks, and how proud she was of him for doing it. But he and Braeden really had avoided the conversation they both knew they had to have. Maybe Mama could shed some light on the thorny problem.

Nudging his mother gently out of the way, Joey reached into the backseat and hefted both of her big suitcases out of the car. "Come on, let's go inside. We'll have dinner, then the three of us can sit down and you can help Braeden and me with our problem."

Mama took her purse and car keys, then led the way to the front porch. As they passed through the garden, Joey felt a fractured thread of thought from a peony with a broken stem. He reached out to it and healed the break, the action as automatic as breathing, and it suddenly struck him how much he'd changed.

In the past few frantic weeks, honing his control over his magic then confronting Caratacus, he hadn't had a chance to think about it. But now, with his subconscious commands turning his mother's little garden into a lush paradise, he realized how different he'd become. Not only from his former self, but from everyone else. How could he continue to live in a world where he no longer fit?

In a way, it made things easier. It narrowed his choices down to the one he'd suspected he'd take all along. But that didn't make it one bit easier to say goodbye.

Nodding to himself, he followed his mother into the house.

೮ঽ

By unspoken agreement, the conversation during dinner steered clear of anything involving Caratacus or magic, or what was going to happen next. They talked about Mama's visit to Texas, about the local scandal involving Fontaine's mayor and several young girls, about the opera Albert had taken Mama to in New Orleans last month. Only when the leftovers had been put away and the dishes washed did Mama sit down, plant her elbows on the table and put on her serious face.

"All right," she said. "We've all had a nice visit, and now I think it's time we all had a talk."

Glancing at Braeden, Joey nodded. "Yeah, we should."

Braeden eased into a chair and sat stiffly on the edge, hands clasped together on the table in front of him. He wore a glamour for the first time in days, and Joey found it disconcerting. He wished Braeden could just be himself, and not worry about making Mama uncomfortable.

"Perhaps first we should tell the tale of Caratacus's defeat," Braeden suggested. "Much has occurred since we last met."

"Yes, I expect so." She turned to Joey, who sat between the other two at the small round table, and patted his hand. "But there's no need to relive anything you don't want to, baby. I know what you had to do down there in South America, and I don't need the details. What I'd most like to know is, what's changed in you, with these new powers of yours? Braeden told me your magic had manifested itself, like I've been afraid it would ever since you were born, but neither of you ever told me what sort of powers you had. What's the faery half of you done to my boy?"

Reaching toward Braeden, Joey took his hand and held on tight. "It all came on me kind of suddenly. I'd been feeling antsy for a few weeks, but on Midsummer I felt like something was coming to a head. I didn't know what it was, but it was like a pressure building up inside me. I left work early that day, and I was walking through the Botanical Gardens when I was hit by this weird feeling. Like something was trying to communicate with me. We were in the middle of a bad drought, and it was like I could feel how much all the plants were suffering."

Realization dawned in his mother's eyes. "You always did have a way with plants. I guess I know why now."

Joey nodded. "It was like something burst inside me that day. I passed out in the Gardens, and when I woke up I was in a cabin in Shining Rock Wilderness, with Braeden."

"Caratacus would have come for him," Braeden explained. "He was only waiting for Joseph's powers to manifest, so that he could find him and—"

"So you said before," Mama interrupted, with a gentle smile. "I'm grateful to you for finding him first, and for all you've done to help him since." She smiled, her sharp gaze searching Braeden's face. "You're meant to be together. I hope you both know that."

Joey's throat went tight. "He has to go back, Mama. He'd stay here if I asked, but that can't happen. They need him in Tir-na-nog. But I...I can't..."

Mama looked at Joey with a knowing sadness in her eyes. "You can't be without him. Right?"

He nodded, unable to speak. Hot tears spilled down his cheeks. Braeden's fingers tightened around his, and he could feel how much his lover wanted to fold him in arms and wings and make it all better. But he wouldn't do it, not with Mama there. Not when they all knew it might be the last time she would ever hold her son.

Rising from her chair, Mama came to Joey and put her arms around his shoulders. He let go of Braeden's hand, wrapped both arms around his mother's waist and rested his head against her bosom.

"It's all right," she crooned, stroking his hair. "It's not an easy choice, but I think you know in your heart what's best. Life's a hard thing, Joseph. It changes us, and sometimes that change makes it impossible to keep living in this world." Curling a finger beneath his chin, she lifted his face to meet her gaze. "You're one of the lucky ones, son. Not everyone has another world to run to, never mind someone there who loves them the way Braeden loves you."

Joey stared up into his mother's face, so familiar and so loved, and knew she was right. But that didn't make it any easier to leave her. "Time's different there, Mama. What if I never see you again?"

Mama's brown eyes clouded, but she smiled anyway. "It'll be hard for both of us, Joseph. But it'll ease my mind to know you're where you belong and you're happy there."

A sob welled up in Joey's throat. He swallowed it, blinking away the tears blurring his vision. Beside him, a chair scraped along the wooden floor, then Braeden's body pressed against his back and Braeden's hands rested on his shoulders.

"The decision is yours, *a chuisle*," Braeden said. "If you wish to remain in the human world, I shall not leave you. I hold to my vow."

Joey leaned his head against Braeden's belly, never looking away from his mother's face. "I've changed too much. I'm a freak here." He let out a bitter laugh. "I didn't tell you this, Braeden, but I cut myself when we were chopping carrots earlier. It healed completely in less than ten minutes."

Mama's eyes widened. "Goodness."

"It is your Sidhe blood," Braeden told him. "All the Fae heal thus, except wounds inflicted by iron."

"Exactly," Joey agreed. "That's just the point. I'm more Sidhe than human now. If I can heal like you do, does that mean I'm immortal too?"

Braeden didn't say anything, but the faint tremor in his hands gave him away. Joey smiled. He couldn't blame

Braeden for wanting him to be immortal. He'd have wanted the same thing if their situations were reversed. Loving a mortal being when you yourself lived forever would be a terrible thing to face.

"I guess I wanted there to be some sort of perfect answer," Joey continued, more to himself than the other two. "But there isn't one. Time's different here and in Tir-na-nog. I could go there for a short visit and hundreds of years might pass here while I'm gone. That means whether Braeden and I stay here or go to Tir-na-nog, we do it together, because neither of us is leaving the other one. Ever."

Mama laid a cool palm on his cheek. Her eyes glittered with gathering moisture. "Oh, baby."

He took her hand and kissed it. "I don't want to leave you, Mama. But I don't belong here anymore."

Her throat worked. He could see her struggling to hold herself together, and it broke his heart. "I know," she said, her voice choked. She gave him a shaky smile. "Will you both stay here with me tonight? I'll fix you breakfast in the morning and see you on your way."

This is it. I'm leaving home again, only it's for good this time. Forever.

The inescapable reality of it hit Joey like a fist in the gut. Robbed of words, he clutched his mother close, his whole body shaking. Behind him, he heard Braeden gravely agree to stay the night. He dropped a kiss on Joey's hair, squeezed his shoulders and walked away.

Secure in the knowledge that his lover wouldn't go far, Joey rested his head on his mother's chest and cried.

Braeden walked out onto the front porch, letting the glamour slip away in the dark. The sounds of Joey's grief, and Evangeline's, hurt him terribly. But they needed this time together. They might never see each other again, and they needed time to say their goodbyes.

He wanted nothing more than the power to make everything right. To create a solution where Tir-na-nog could be put to rights, where he and Joseph could live carefree and happy here in the human world, and Joseph would not have to leave behind his home and his only family. But no such magic existed in all the worlds, and he knew Joseph's choice was the right one. This world would bring his love nothing but grief now. In Tir-na-nog, Joseph could be happy, and his magic could blossom to its full potential.

Perhaps he will even get his wings.

The thought made Braeden smile. Wings—real wings, ones that could bear him aloft and let him soar through the summer sky—would be a delight beyond compare to Joseph.

Wandering out to the spot where he and Joseph had made love the previous day, Braeden breathed in the scent of damp earth and honeysuckle and let the peacefulness seep into him. Crickets chirped in the grass and fireflies blinked in the shadows under the trees.

The little golden lights called to him. And after all, how often did one get the chance to frolic with the fireflies?

Braeden gathered his magic to him and sent a pulse through his body. The soft blue light flashed through him, and the change was complete. Taking wing, Braeden fluttered off to join the throng under the trees.

C33

Joey and his mother sat up talking the rest of the night. They ended up working through lots of things they'd never spoken of before. By the time the sky outside began to pale with the coming dawn, Joey felt closer to her than he ever had, and he'd made his peace with leaving.

His mother shooed him out of the kitchen while she cooked breakfast. Yawning, he wandered into the living room to find Braeden, but he wasn't there.

"Must've gone upstairs," Joey muttered to himself. Braeden certainly knew where his room was. Joey smiled, remembering that long-ago night when Braeden had kissed his brow and bound them together.

He climbed the stairs and opened the door of his room, expecting to find Braeden waiting for him. The room was empty. Unease fluttered in his belly for a second before his good sense reasserted itself. Braeden loved flying in the first morning light. He was probably outside.

Joey crossed the room, opened the window and leaned on the sill. The cool air rang with birdsong and the rustle of leaves in the light breeze. Joey smiled when he saw the lone firefly lingering under the stand of oaks. That tiny point of light wasn't quite what it seemed. And he belonged to Joey.

As if sensing his thoughts, the firefly left the shelter of the trees and drifted up to the open window. Joey moved aside. The tiny creature floated inside, the familiar blue light pulsed, and Braeden stood there, every bit as beautiful as he'd been twenty years before.

"Is all well?" Braeden pulled Joey to him, silver-gray eyes searching his face. "Is Evangeline all right? And you, Joseph?"

"We're both fine." Joey smiled as Braeden's wings folded around him. "It's funny, you know. I never realized how many things we'd never said to each other that we really should've. Now that we've talked through all those things, we both feel better about me leaving."

Cupping Joey's cheek in one hand, Braeden kissed his lips. "You are so very strong, my love. So brave."

"I'm only doing what I have to," Joey protested, blushing. "That's all I did with Caratacus, and that's all I'm doing now. That's not brave."

Braeden smiled. "That is the bravest thing of all."

The love in Braeden's eyes made Joey feel warm right to his core. Slipping both arms around Braeden's neck, Joey lifted his face for a kiss.

Mama's voice calling their names broke them apart. "Breakfast must be ready," Joey said, nipping at Braeden's lower lip.

"Apparently so." Raising his head, Braeden drew a deep breath. "It smells magnificent."

"Yeah. Let's go eat, huh?" *My last breakfast with my mother.* Grief dug its sharp claws into Joey's gut, but he ignored it. He was determined to enjoy his last moments with Mama, and leave her with the knowledge that he was happy.

"Of course." Braeden pressed a kiss to his hair. "I love you, Joseph. Now, and always."

"I love you too." Joey smiled, fingers caressing one gossamer wing where it curved around his body. He drew out of Braeden's arms and took his hand. "Come on. Mama's making waffles."

Braeden nodded, lacing their fingers together, and they went downstairs hand in hand.

α

They lingered over breakfast for another couple of hours, talking while they ate Mama's delicious homemade waffles and fresh fruit from the farmer's market down the road. Joey and his mother talked candidly about what might happen once Joey left.

He could tell Braeden was surprised but happy they were being so up front about the whole thing. Joey was happy about it himself. It was a huge relief to speak openly with his mother about how they both felt, rather than try to hide it.

"We're going to come back," Joey said, covering Mama's hand with his. "We'll be very careful, though. We'll both be glamoured, just in case."

"That's for the best." She gazed at him with sadness in her eyes. "I won't let myself expect to see you again, Joey. There's too much chance it won't happen, and I won't get my hopes up."

"I know. I'm not getting my hopes up either." Joey tried to mean it, but he knew it was a lie. He couldn't help hoping. "When we come back, we'll come here."

"I'm not going anywhere." Mama's expression turned unusually shy. "Honey, there's something I didn't tell you last night."

Fear clutched at Joey's chest, though he had no idea why. "What is it?"

"Nothing bad, baby, don't worry." Smiling, Mama took his hand in both of hers. "Before you showed up last week, Albert asked me to marry him."

Shocked, Joey could only blink at her. "What? He did what?"

She laughed. "He was here the night before you two came here, and he asked me to marry him. I didn't know where you were or what had happened to you, or how Caratacus was involved in it all, and I couldn't think of anything else until I knew. I told him I needed time to think. He knew you were missing, and he knew how much that tore me up, so he agreed to give me time."

"And what will your answer be?" Braeden asked, breaking the silence he'd kept for the last few minutes.

Mama's face softened into a look Joey hadn't seen since his father—his real one, the one who'd raised him and loved him—was alive. "I'm going to tell him yes."

Gazing into his mother's eyes, Joey saw a joyful future for her, and was glad. He flung his arms around her and hugged her hard. "That's wonderful, Mama. I'm so happy for you." He pulled back, a smile spreading across his face. "Albert's a good guy. I like him."

"Yes, he's a good man." Mama patted his cheek, her eyes shining. "I've been lonely since your father died. Albert's good to me. He loves me."

"Do you love him, Mama?" The answer was plain on Mama's face, but Joey needed to hear her say it before he could rest easy.

She nodded. "I'll never love anyone the way I did Robert Vines. That man was special. But I do love Albert, yes." Laying her hands on Joey's cheeks, she leaned forward and kissed his brow. "I'll be happy, baby. Don't you worry about me."

"Okay, I won't worry," he promised, and it was true. "Same here, yeah? I'll be happy in Tir-na-nog. It won't be like it was with Caratacus alive."

"I'm glad of that." Letting go of Joey, Mama stood and began gathering the dirty dishes. "I suppose you boys need to be on your way."

Joey's chest tightened. This time, it was excitement about what lay ahead making his hands tremble and his pulse race. He glanced at Braeden. "Yeah, I guess so. Braeden, should we go outside?"

"There is no need. I can open a portal from here." Moving forward, Braeden laid his hands on Mama's shoulders and kissed both her cheeks. "Be happy, Evangeline. You have earned it."

"Thank you." A tear spilled over her cheek, and she wiped it away. "You take care of my baby, okay?"

"Always. You have my promise."

As soon as Braeden stepped back, Joey flung himself into his mother's arms. He closed his eyes and pressed his cheek to hers. Both their faces were damp with tears, but he could tell she was at peace with the situation, and he knew he himself was. They would both be fine.

"Goodbye, Mama," he whispered. "I love you."

"I love you too, sweetheart." She pulled back, her smile radiant. "Goodbye."

Letting go was hard, but Joey had a whole new life waiting for him in a world he had yet to see. He took Braeden's hand in his. "I'm ready."

Behind him, Joey heard the now-familiar crackle of a portal opening. He held his mother's gaze, and they smiled at each other as the portal drew him in.

The first thing Braeden did when he and Joseph stepped from the portal into Tir-na-nog was dissolve the glamour he'd been wearing, as well as Joseph's clothing. They needed neither here.

He glanced around. The emerald hills and cerulean sky were exactly as he remembered. He wriggled his bare toes in the cool grass and breathed deep. The air of his home, untainted by the industries which polluted the human world, smelled sweet and clean. A soft, warm breeze fanned his face, bringing with it the sounds of lutes and singing from somewhere on the other side of the nearby rise.

I'm home. At last. He was glad to be here, for certain, but the thought reminded him that Joseph had left everything behind to come here with him.

He turned and framed Joseph's face in his hands, staring deep into his eyes. "It is done, my love. Are you all right?"

Nodding, Joseph brushed a light kiss across his mouth. "I'm fine. This place is..." He glanced around, dark eyes alight with wonder. "God, it's amazing. Beautiful."

"That it is." Braeden rested his forehead against Joseph's. "I am sorry you had to leave your home, *a chuisle.* I would change that if I could."

Joseph smiled, fingers combing through Braeden's hair. "You can't, though. And neither can I. And I'm glad I can be here with you. I've always wanted to see this place, you know. Ever since I was a kid."

"Then I am happy I could fulfill that wish, my love."

"Me too." Joseph pressed closer, his smile turning seductive. "Kiss me."

Braeden obeyed, burying one hand in Joseph's hair and sliding the other down to cup his ass. Joseph opened to him with a sigh.

As often happened between them, the kiss grew deep and heated, finesse all but lost in their hunger for one another. Braeden slid a finger into Joseph's crease to tease his hole. To his shock, Joseph yelped and stiffened in his arms.

"Joseph?" He drew back enough to study Joseph's face. The man's mouth was drawn into a rictus of pain. Sweat beaded on his brow, and his skin had gone a strange shade of gray under his natural dark coloring. Fear clutched at Braeden's stomach. "Joseph, love, what ails you? Did...did I hurt you?"

Joseph shook his head. "No," he said through clenched teeth. "It's my back. It just...just hurts like hell all of a sudden. Feels like...like something's under my skin, trying to get out. Had it the...the day you found me, just an itching, then it went away after... Fuck! After my powers appeared."

Suddenly Braeden knew what it was. It had been many hundreds of years since he'd felt that agony himself. He'd nearly forgotten.

"It's all right, my love," he said, giving Joseph a reassuring smile. "It's simply—"

Joseph's gut-wrenching scream cut him off. He managed to catch Joseph as his knees buckled and lower him gently to the ground. Joseph curled into a ball, his entire body shaking as if in the grip of a violent fever.

Braeden knelt beside him, caressing the spot where the skin between his shoulder blades bulged outward in two irregular lumps.

"Hurts, Braeden," Joseph whimpered. "God, what is it?"

"It's your wings, *a chuisle*," Braeden answered, and kissed Joseph's cheek. "You are growing wings."

Joseph blinked, his expression reflecting stunned surprise. He licked his lips, looking as though he were about to speak. Then the skin of his back split, and he shrieked as the wings erupted from his body. There was very little blood, the flesh healing in an instant.

Braeden stared, struck dumb by the beauty of his love's new appendages. Translucent silver-white, they shimmered with iridescent color in the sunlight. Reaching out, Braeden stroked a careful finger down the damp, curled edge of one wing. It quivered at his touch.

"I felt that." Joseph's voice was full of wonder. "It feels... I don't know what it feels like. But I like it."

"Are you in pain still?" Sitting cross-legged on the ground, Braeden brushed the hair from Joseph's face. "It has been many centuries since my wings came in, but I do not think the pain lasted once they broke free of my skin."

"No, it doesn't hurt now." Joseph pushed himself to a sitting position, his face screwed up in concentration. "Damn. How do you learn to move around without hurting them?"

"Within a few days, the movements will be instinctive, and you will no longer think about it." Braeden smiled, watching the riot of emotion flowing across Joseph's face as his wings unfurled behind him, drying quickly in the balmy breeze. "They are much tougher than they look, and not easily torn or damaged."

"That makes sense. If they weren't, you couldn't fly with them, I guess." Joseph twisted his head around, obviously trying to get a good look at his wings. "Wow. They're pretty."

"They are beautiful." Planting a hand in the thick green grass, Braeden leaned over to kiss Joseph's lips. "*You* are beautiful, my love."

"Sweet talker." Joseph nipped Braeden's lip. "Hey, what are those little flowers in the grass? The blue ones?"

Braeden glanced down at the tiny flowers sprinkling the meadow in which they lay. The round, vivid blue blossoms each held a teardrop-shaped pistil of a blue so pale it was nearly white. "They are called Maiden's Tears. They are common, but well loved. The maidens of the kingdom love to wear them in their hair, believing they drive away sorrow."

Joseph's eyes took on a teasing sparkle. He grinned, and Braeden let out a soft cry of surprise when he felt something slither up his back and wind into his hair. A flash of blue told him it was Maiden's Tears, growing swift as thought into his hair, the long stems breaking off and curling back into the grass once the flower had found its place.

"Joseph, what are you doing?" he demanded, trying without success to look stern. He gently tugged a delicate green stem from behind his ear and held up the little blue bloom. "I am not a maiden, love."

"I know, but they wanted to be in your hair." Rising to his knees, Joseph scooted closer and slid his arms around Braeden's neck. "They have a really strong voice, you know. I wonder if the girls don't put them in their hair because they're responding to what the flowers want. They seem to like being decoration."

Laughing, Braeden touched a fingertip to one of the blossoms which had insinuated itself into Joseph's own tresses. The pure, clear blue shone like bits of gemstone against the ebony waves. "Your magic is stronger here, love. I can feel it. And now that you are here, you will likely develop new powers. Soon none in the kingdom would dare stand against you."

The sparkle went out of Joseph's eyes, replaced by a grave seriousness. "I don't want it to be like that, Braeden. I don't want power over anybody else. All I want is for you and me to be together and happy. We don't need much for that."

"Absolutely." Braeden stretched up to claim a kiss, then rose to his feet. "Come. On the other side of that hill is the home of my captain. He and his wife guard the secret of the Prince's hiding place. We must speak to them, and bring them the good news. They will likely have heard your screams when your wings came through, so we may meet someone on the way."

Joseph glanced at the round hilltop as he stood. "Can we fly there?"

Braeden considered. "Quite possibly. Your wings should be dry enough to attempt it by now. It takes a bit of practice to learn your balance in the air, and the muscles will be sore at first until they gain strength, but I believe—"

The whoosh of Joseph's wings beating the air for the first time dried the words in Braeden's throat. Joseph hovered a couple of feet above the ground, wings fluttering just enough to keep him aloft. A wide smile glowed on his face.

"Come on, Braeden," Joseph said, holding a hand out and nearly tumbling to the ground in the process. "Let's go."

Laughing, Braeden took Joseph's hand—carefully, so as not to upset his precarious balance—and rose slowly into the air. Joseph wobbled, bit his lip and regained his composure. Steady now in the air, he intertwined his fingers with Braeden's and beamed at him.

"You're doing beautifully," Braeden said. He squeezed Joseph's hand. "Welcome home, my love."

The light in Joseph's eyes said all the things he didn't voice. Hand in hand, they took wing.

Epilogue

The portal crackled, and Joey stepped out into a bog which hadn't been there before. He rose into the hot, humid air just as Braeden emerged from the portal behind him. Raising an eyebrow, Braeden fluttered aloft beside him.

"Can you find her, love?" Braeden asked, scanning a horizon lost in grayish haze in one direction and swallowed by abnormally tall mangroves in the other. "Everything has changed. More so than I ever would have suspected."

Joey nodded, his throat tight. "Yes. She's right where we left her. It just looks different, that's all."

Braeden didn't say anything, but Joey knew he believed him. He was sure he had the location right. This had been a stand of oak trees once upon a time, guarding a rambling white farmhouse with a small but colorful garden. Fifty paces behind the house, between two gnarled willows, lay a grave with a Celtic cross headstone reading simply "Evangeline". Forget-me-nots twined around the stone, and violets dotted the grass in spring.

Joey had placed that marker at the head of his mother's grave with his own hands, and set her favorite flowers to grow there. He'd wound enchantments around the place, to keep the flowers growing and the stone intact. He had no doubt he could find it again, even though the landscape had changed so drastically.

Rising higher into the air, Joey drifted above the green bog, feeling for the traces of his own magic in the earth. Braeden flew by his side, looking around with furrowed brow and thoughtful gaze. A grayish-white fish leapt from the dark water and re-entered it with a plop. The sound seemed magnified in the strange, still silence.

"Why is it so quiet?" Joey wondered, frowning at the rippling surface of the bog below him. "I don't hear any insects, or any birds."

"No cars, either," Braeden pointed out. "Or airplanes."

Surprised, Joey glanced up at him. "You're right. There were always mechanical sounds before. You could even hear the hum of the power lines. That's all gone now."

"I wonder how much time has passed since last we visited this place," Braeden mused. "It has been many long years in Tir-na-nog. Millennia could have gone by here."

A familiar ache lodged itself in Joey's chest. In fact, more than two hundred years had passed in Tir-na-nog since they'd last been here. He and Braeden had returned to the human world barely a week after arriving in Tir-na-nog, only to find his mother widowed for a second time and dying alone in the house where Joey had grown up. Joey had been shocked to discover that almost sixty years had passed here, and his mother was over one hundred years old. She'd died in her own bed, holding Joey's hand, and he and Braeden had buried her in the land she'd loved in life.

Braeden had said she'd only been waiting to see Joey one last time. Whether it was true or not, it brought him a measure of comfort to be with his mother at the moment of her death, and he knew his presence had given her comfort as well.

A tingle of magic pulled at Joey's insides. Hovering inches above the bog, he squinted through the water. Something pale wavered just beneath the surface. He waved his hand and murmured a few words in Gaelic. A whirlpool formed and swiftly expanded, revealing a worn Celtic cross and a patch of sodden silt. He laid a palm on the stone. It was slick with slime and strangely warm.

Beside him, Braeden spoke a drying spell which turned the muck below them into solid earth. They settled side by side before the grave marker.

"Hi, Mama." Sinking to his knees, Joey thought the covering of algae away and brushed his fingers over his mother's name carved in the stone. "I'm sorry it took me so long to come back. After you died, there just didn't seem to be any point in returning."

He stared up into the veiled sky, fighting the hollow sensation in his chest. Seeing his former home so changed—so silent and empty—was even harder than knowing Mama was no longer here. "Everything's good for me, Mama. Braeden and I have a nice quiet life in Tir-na-nog. At first everybody treated me like some big hero—"

"Because you are, love," Braeden interrupted, laying his hands on Joey's shoulders.

Smiling, Joey reached his free hand back and wound his fingers through Braeden's. "But after a while they settled down, and now they treat me like a regular person—well, a regular faery—and that's how I like it. King Donovan's a good ruler. Braeden says he's just like his mother, Queen Brigitta. Everyone loves him. I think of you all the time, Mama. I miss you, and I miss this place, but..."

A lump rose in Joey's throat. Tears welled in his eyes, turning the headstone, the water and the trees, into a glittering blur. He blinked the moisture away. Letting go of Braeden's hand, he planted both palms on the cross and leaned forward until his forehead rested against the cool, damp stone.

"Tir-na-nog is my home now," he continued at last. "It's a beautiful place, and a happy place now without Caratacus. And Braeden is everything I need."

Behind him, Braeden sank to the ground and wound an arm around his shoulders. Joey leaned against him, grateful for his lover's solid presence. "I'm happy, Mama," he said softly. "Wherever you are now, whether you can hear me or not, I hope you're happy too." He glanced around, shivering a little in spite of the heat. The thick, waiting silence was oppressive. "I don't think we'll be coming back here anymore."

He sat there for a few minutes, safe in the curve of Braeden's arm, lost in thought. He wasn't sure why he'd been compelled to come back here now, after staying away for so long. Maybe he couldn't really let go of his former home until all traces of his mother were gone and it had changed beyond all recognition.

That day, it seemed, had arrived. His own magic still lingered around Mama's grave, but he sensed none of her essence here. Her spirit was gone, her body long since absorbed into the earth. Nothing was left of the place where a barefoot little boy had once talked to hollow trees and held fireflies in his cupped hands on summer evenings.

Joey pushed to his feet, Braeden standing alongside him. He took Braeden's hand. "I'm ready to go now."

Braeden glanced at him as they rose into the breathless air. "Is that it, then? Is this the last we shall see of your world?"

"This isn't my world anymore, Braeden. Even the plants feel different. I can barely understand them. I don't know what's happened to this place. But it's not mine anymore." Hovering in midair, Joey took one last look around, then turned to Braeden. "Let's go home."

Without a word, Braeden opened a portal for them. Joey saw a dragonfly nearly as large as himself buzz past before the portal closed and the sad, silent world he'd once called home vanished.

A split second later, an oval of soft lavender light opened and spilled them back into the land of the Sidhe. Joey breathed deep of the fragrant evening air, feeling the tension drain from his body. This was indeed his home now. He belonged here, in a land that welcomed everything he was, with a love who would be by his side for all time.

Braeden snuggled behind him, arms around his waist, and kissed his neck. "Look, Joseph."

Joey looked in the direction Braeden indicated. A small crowd of the younger Fae were gathered in a nearby hollow of the rolling hills. A few whirled in a complicated midair dance, laughing with their bell-like voices. Several had transformed into fireflies and were busy weaving a swirling pattern of golden light in the dusk.

Ever since the first faery child had caught Braeden transforming into one of the tiny creatures, playing Fireflies had become a hugely popular game among the high-spirited youngsters. Joey blamed Braeden, who had readily agreed to teach the trick he'd learned in the world of humans.

Not that Joey had room to talk, really. He'd been just as eager to learn himself, and spending time looking at the world through firefly eyes had become a daily ritual for him and Braeden.

Joey turned in Braeden's arms and kissed him. "Want to go play?"

Braeden's wide smile lit up the dark. "Certainly." Giving Joey a smack on the butt, he drew away from the embrace and rose into the air with a few strong beats of his wings. "Come along, love," he called, and shot off toward the crowd of children, who had by now spotted them and were calling them over.

Laughing, Joey took to the air in Braeden's wake. He transformed as he flew, and joined the galaxy of living light twinkling in the grass.

About the Author

Ally Blue used to be a good girl. Really. Married for twenty years, two lovely children, house, dogs, picket fence, the whole deal. Then one day she discovered slash fan fiction. She wrote her first fan fiction story a couple of months later and has since slid merrily into the abyss. She has had several short stories published in the erotic e-zine Ruthie's Club, and is a regular contributor to the original slash e-zine Forbidden Fruit.

To learn more about Ally Blue, please visit www.allyblue.com. Send an email to Ally at ally@allyblue.com or join her Yahoo! group to join in the fun with other readers as well as Ally! http://groups.yahoo.com/group/loveisblue/.

Look for these titles by
Ally Blue

Now Available:

Willow Bend

Love's Evolution

Oleander House:
Book One of the Bay City Paranormal Investigation Series

Eros Rising

Hearts from the Ashes
(Paperback collection which includes Eros Rising)

What Hides Inside:
Book Two of the Bay City Paranormal Investigation Series

Catching a Buzz

Coming Soon:

Twilight:
Book Three of the Bay City Paranormal Investigation Series

Untamed Heart

Closer:
Book Four of the Bay City Paranormal Investigation Series

Where the Heart Is

The Happy Onion

An Inner Darkness:
Book Five of the Bay City Paranormal Investigation Series

hot stuff

Discover Samhain!

Can a straight-laced business student and an indie boy with a thing for extremely personal electronics turn one night's wild ride into a trip to last forever?

Catching a Buzz
© *2007 Ally Blue*

Adam Holderman isn't your typical twenty-something college boy. He prefers jazz to Goth, shuns body piercings and street-waif clothing, and despises the lack of vocabulary among his peers. Some call him uptight, but Adam doesn't see it that way. Just because he prefers his men articulate and well-groomed doesn't make him a stick-in-the-mud. He simply has standards, unlike most guys his age.

The new employee at Wild Waters Park, where Adam works, single-handedly throws a monkey wrench into Adam's orderly world view. Buzz Stiles wears eyeliner and black clothes, listens to emo bands, and talks like a teenage skate punk. He's the polar opposite of Adam's avowed "type". So why can't Adam get him out of his head?

When Adam finally agrees to go out with Buzz, he finds there's much more to Buzz than a hot body, a sharp wit, and a Goth fashion sense. Buzz is someone Adam can see himself being with for the long haul. But you need more than mind-melting sex to make a relationship last. Can they keep their hands off each other long enough to find out if they have what it takes?

Warning, this title contains the following: graphic language, explicit male/male sex, inappropriate use of personal electronic devices, and gratuitous disco dancing.

Available now in ebook from Samhain Publishing.

Talk about a compromising situation!

My Fair Captain
© 2007 J.L. Langley

A storm of political intrigue, murderous mayhem and sexual hungers is brewing on planet Regelence.

Swarthy Intergalactic Navy Captain Nathaniel Hawkins ran from a past he had no intention of ever reliving. But when his Admiral asks him to use his peerage, as an earl and the heir to a dukedom, to investigate a missing weapons stash, he's forced to do just that. As if being undercover on a Regency planet where the young men are supposed to remain pure until marriage isn't bad enough, Nate finds himself attracted to the king's unmarried son.

All Prince Aiden Townsend has ever wanted was to be an artist. He has no interest in a marriage of political fortune or becoming a societal paragon. Until he lands in the arms of the mysterious Earl of Deverell. One look at Nate's handsome face has Aiden reconsidering his future. Not only does Nate make a virile subject for Aiden's art, but the great war hero awakens feelings in Aiden he has never felt, feelings he can't ignore.

After a momentous dance at a season ball, Aiden and Nate find themselves exchanging important information and working closely together. They have to fight their growing attraction long enough to find out who stole the weapons and keep themselves from a compromising situation and certain scandal.

Warning, this title contains the following: explicit sex, graphic language, violence, hot nekkid man-love.

Available now in ebook and print from Samhain Publishing.

Printed in the United States
112418LV00001B/244-276/P